You have written the history of Odia middle class and a fragile joint family in your novel Nabalak (The Minor) which made me cry only! I have a feeling that you have written about me in this novel. I am as helpless as you after losing my mother. Let all your creative work achieve all possible heights

Debraj Lenka , *Eminent Writer*

I have ploughed a *Maana* (1/4th of an acre), let you cultivate a *baati* (four acres of land). Your book 'Nabalak' (The Minor) is the contemporary history of our ever-fragile home. You are the inheritor of my creative world. All my blessings to you for your future.

Late Mohapatra Nilamani Sahu, *Eminent Writer*

The theme and storyline of Nabalak (The Minor) encompass the love, care, and suffering of a broken, joint family which will probably be never written in any history book. So someone may call 'Nabalak (The Minor) a literature piece and history by many others.

Alok Sadhangi

The history of our time… blended with stories of our childhood days… One of the best sellers in Odia Literature.

The Minor

Odia Novel: NABALAK

Ajay Swain

Translated by

Dr. Tapan K Panda

BLACK EAGLE BOOKS

Dublin, USA | Bhubaneswar, India

 Black Eagle Books
USA address:
7464 Wisdom Lane
Dublin, OH 43016

India address:
E/312, Trident Galaxy, Kalinga Nagar,
Bhubaneswar-751003, Odisha, India

E-mail: info@blackeaglebooks.org
Website: www.blackeaglebooks.org

First International Edition Published by
Black Eagle Books, 2023

THE MINOR
(Odia Novel: Nabalak)
by **Ajay Swain**

Translated by **Dr. Tapan K Panda**

Original Copyright © Ajay Swain
Translation Copyright © Dr. Tapan K Panda

Cover & Interior Design: Ezy's Publication

ISBN- 978-1-64560-455-6 (Paperback)
Library of Congress Control Number: 2023947597

Printed in the United States of America

This translation is dedicated to friends of my minor days - Shantanu Patnaik, Krushna Acharya, Surendra Moharana, Avay Rath, Deepak Patel, Lalita Panda, Pushpa Kar, Sharada Padhi, Haramani Behera and inhabitants of a small colony called 'Biswabanshi Colony' .in Khurdha Road where I had spent my minor days

- Dr Tapan K Panda

The Idea of Our Childhood

The Minor (Nabalak) is the story of the metamorphosis of the protagonist. The memories of who he was and where he lived are important to him. When he was a child, he seldom thought of the future. This innocence left him free to enjoy as few adults can. The day he frets about the future is when he leaves his childhood behind.

The truth of life is that we get farther away from the essence that is born within us. We get shouldered with burdens, things happen to us, loved ones die, and people lose their way for a reason or another. It's not hard to do in this world of crazy mazes. Life does its best to take that memory of magic away from us. You don't know it's happening until one day we feel we have lost something, but you are not sure what it is. Childhood, after all, is the first precious coin.

'The Minor' is one of the difficult projects that I have recently worked on. As I have mentioned earlier, I only work on a book when I like reading it as a reader and not as a translator. I have refused the work of many other established writers because the books didn't appeal to me. This project is difficult on two counts: the original book has so many words which are colloquial and hardly there are English equivalents available; the second point is about the structure and flow. The prose is written in such a poetic flow; I have struggled in a few places. This is natural as Ajay Bhai is a terrific poet and he brings that poetic brilliance into his fictional writing.

I am a big fan of Ajay Swain – the writer for almost four decades now. I have spent many golden moments of my life with him in the early nineties when I was in Odisha. This time when I planned to translate one of his works- I had to choose from all his brilliant work and I decided to work on this classic piece- the most published and talked about book of the last thirty years. I am thankful to Sri Ajay Swain for kindly consenting to translate this work. I am sure the new generation of readers (at least half a dozen of them have read this manuscript and commented on the translation) will like to experience our childhood days and long for its beauty as they grow old. I have dedicated 'The Minor' to my minor day friends. I thank them for enriching my life with their varied interactions with me during my growing-up years.

I am thankful to Sri Satya Patnaik of Black Eagle Books for kindly agreeing and publishing the translated version of one of the most popular, much talked about, and appreciated book 'Nabalak; Sri Ashok Parida for his cover and book design. I am hopeful that the translated version of Nabalak will reach the same height among English readers as the original.

Dr Tapan K Panda
23rd August, 2023

Where will I begin from?

From where I should go about... From where... from where shall I? Shall I start with the raindrops dribbling down the thatched roof in a runnel conjuring my memories of making little paper boats and putting them to float on the water or my aunt *Kana* who hanged herself on a tree because of premarital pregnancy in the mid of the night on the bank of the river *Dayaa* and became a hag? She sits on the tree, hanging her legs with a mouth like a fireplace and a chimney for a nose, or shall I begin with sprinting on the bank of the river or in the moonlit night among the flowering field, pale like melting gold as it swept across miles and miles of even land?

Even though I continue to write, it's never-ending as the sequence of events, happenings, characters, and a thousand recollections weave their air threads into woof. The perpetual heart throbbing, spine-chilling pathos penetrates the bones, and the heart reverberates – Alas!

I couldn't express one thing: how people addressed my widowed grandmother as a witch. I surreptitiously saw her taking a bath every night and chewing the *Tulsi (Holi Basil Plant)* leaves as she was edgy. Still, the villagers said that she was a hag who fed on human excrement.

One of my friends, *Nanda*, in fifth grade with me while singing, had excruciating pain in his abdomen and collapsed. I didn't write about my mother's diary, where she noted down the songs and kept the letter she wrote to my father but could never post. I couldn't write how my Mathematics teacher, *Bira* sir, used to tell us the story of *Shravan Kumar* while teaching. He had a unique style of narrating, and till now, I have never heard anyone like his storytelling skills. I also didn't write about *Jayi's* uncle, who always had dinner in our house at night so that he could narrate the stories to me. His stories were never-ending, but I was growing older and older listening to them. (Ah! The sweet old days when I was a minor).

My father's name was *Shri Anaam Charan Swain*; he is no longer there but was the first reader of my stories. I pay tribute to my father, writer, and novelist Shri *Mahapatra Nilamani Sahu*, who was fascinated after reading my novel' *Kutaa Khiyakara Ghara* (The House of Straw)' and gave me the status of being his prodigal son.

It's a tribute to Odisha's fascinating, magical, and renowned writer-novelist, *Shri Debraj Lenka*, with whom I have prayed, loved, got angry with, and taken pride in being with him. Together, we have seen the moonlit nights on the banks of the rivers *Mahanadi* and *Dayaa*. *Drunk*, we have listened to the song of Begum Akhtar.

> ***Mere hum-nafas, mere hum-navaa,***
> *mujhe dost banake dagaa na de*
> *mai.n huu.N dard-e-ishq se jaa.nivalab,*
> *mujhe zindagii kii duaa na de*

You're counting me as a friend when I consider you my life; it feels nothing short of a betrayal.

This love has brought me to the brink of a beautiful death. Don't, please don't pray that I stay well.

Sometimes, we have sat on the seashore mesmerized by the scent of hair and perfume; we have wept inside the *Charchika* temple. And some other times, I have turned into the character of *Abdulla Deewana* in his stories. I dedicate all the breaths of my adult days to him.

Once I hold a pen, the images of those friends that came running into my mind, amazed me, and inspired me include poet *Purna Chandra Maharana*, writer and novelist *Gourahari Das*, poet *Sudha Dash*, poet *Akhil Nayak, Suresh Balabantray, Akshaya Swain*, artist *Kishore Rath, Sanjay Dasbarma, Pushpa Das, Pravati Satpathy;* friend *Rajaniranjan Dash*, writer novelist *Dr Abhay Barik* and poet *Bharat Majhi.* I reminisce about all of them from the core of my heart.

A significant chapter of my adult days would have remained incomplete without 'Aru', who is still alive in my memories and takes life from these memories and turns from a picture into a character; I dedicate all the pages of my adulthood to Aru.

I received over three hundred letters after my two novels were published in «Chitra" and "Sucharita". I am thankful to all my well-wishers' and readers.

While writing this novel, I often behaved like a child and cried. The one who wiped my tears on her veil wiped them on her palms and sang the lullabies of a dense maize field (now turning into darkness from stone). My sleep and silence are only for her.

My heartfelt gratitude to the poet friend who took the responsibility of publishing the first edition of this novel, editor of *'Biswamukti' Sashaank Chudamani,* to whom I enthusiastically narrated the dreams of my elder uncle, mother, and the river *Lunaa;* the young poet *Sudhir Maudamani* who experiences the life and the dreams of youth through the hymn of life are the two who brought the darkness of my minor days into the limelight. My cuddle to both.

Then there are four of them left. Instead of being a writer, if I had become mine worker, then they would have always felt proud of me; among them, one is the poet, writer, and legislator *Dr Dilip Srichandan;* the second one is the editor of 'Ajigarta', poet *Bijay Behura;* and the third one is my younger brother and writer, poet *Akshaya Swain.* Finally, my mother, who has never read my writings. Then, my better half, Asima Swain, stood by me like a rock when my absentmindedness would have orphaned my emotions.

Other than them are my readers, who have appreciated, criticized, and searched for my writings in magazines and books.

Ajay Swain

Everybody has a Childhood

(Preface to the English Edition)

So also I had mine! I was proud of the same childhood (I am sure it's not me alone, but everyone must have that sense of pride). I had never considered writing something like this based on my childhood memoir. It is always a pleasure to live those moments as your own. One recalls everything- from the simplicity of those naughty days to your teenage years, where every season turns into seasons of love. Whenever I start writing about those minor incidents and accidents, I experience a feeling as if I am penning down middle-class *Odisha*'s history. There will be a time when all these will go into oblivion, and then these incidents will turn into historical events for gen-next writers and authors.

I didn't write '*Nabaalak*' as an author's duty. While writing, I wished the readers to enjoy the novel and identify themselves as characters. Spread over five decades, the incidents and feelings (as if they were not mine alone but of Odisha's all middle class) roamed around me, and, like my parents, I never wanted to be a celebrity or even published. I have only transcribed their self-appraisals and confessions into pages.

Being translated into English now, this will be the tenth edition of the novel. I thank eminent contemporary writer Dr. Tapan K Panda for translating this novel. I am obliged to all the characters who have mesmerized me while writing *Nabaalak-* In other words; I am obliged to the characters from whom I have borrowed this writing — my sincere gratitude to Black Eagle Books for taking the responsibility of publishing the book.

Ajay Swain

CHAPTER-1

The prince is waiting near the riverbank- Oh, Yes! Asking me for the gold bangles- Oh Yes!
Make the gold bangles- Oh Yes!
Throw it into the water.
Give me a pound of flesh…!

My grandmother, who said this is now a twinkling star in the sky. She said: After death, the dead becomes a star. The stars you see twinkling in the sky are nothing but the eyes of dead people.

The stories of my grandmother revolved around spirits and ghosts. She said: The ghosts and spirits wander around the villages, and these ghostly apparitions are frightened of the village deity who otherwise looks like a black pained stone, smeared with turmeric and vermilion, and has brass, beaming eyes. The village goddess subjugates them; otherwise, the goddesses responsible for Cholera, Chickenpox, and Ditheism would have shown their tyranny to our and other close-by villagers.

Sulli's mother, often possessed by the village deity, is now dead. Still, we couldn't distinguish which one among those twinkling stars was the eyes of the goddesses.

Sulli's mother was possessed by the village goddesses at least three to four times a year. She bellowed in the village street when possessed, and the hoot of her laughter sacred the small kids like us, and we tried to hide behind the door. She visited different places in the village and nearby villages with a cane in her hand and inhaled the incense.

My elder uncle, an oratorio singer, would sing pleasantly: Dear friend, swear by me and say....

Who is she?

Sulli's mother would scream and says: Don't you know who I am? Are you mocking me? I will count and take seven hundred heads. Look! I swear.

After that, she would place the burning wicks in her mouth. She would blink her eyes, smack her lips, and lose her consciousness. She recuperates when the water is sprinkled on her and then covers her face with a handful of a veil.

My elder uncle was her elderly brother-in-law. He would return with his group of oratorio singers, and I would follow them. I would ask my elder uncle about *Sulli*'s mother's behavior because it always startled me.

My uncle would laugh and say: Try to understand. As we are human beings, so are the Gods. As humans, we are bound by earthly pleasure; they also have. Human beings are the creation of God. Sometimes to test the human being, Gods incarnate in this mortal world.

I could never understand what he said.

I asked my uncle: What are you saying? I am unable to understand.

My uncle would say: Boy! These are mystical knowledge. You can only understand and achieve it if you practice and meditate. Your bookish knowledge will never help with this. You need to concentrate and meditate. Many saints have become anthills during meditation and have suffered greatly by entering different mortal bodies. It is a highly mystifying subject. If you can understand *Brahma* (supreme soul), you can appreciate its mystery.

I would keep thinking about what was told to me for a long time but could never understand it. *Saakhi Apaa* (sister), my cousin, died, and on her death news, my uncle lamented, turned into a rock, and finally left this mortal world. Till now I have never been able e a single line of his words!

Of course, my father didn't want me to get into this matter. Sometimes I would ask my father during his sleeping hours: Father, elder uncle spoke about the divine knowledge; what is that?

My father always laughed and said: That's not a part of what to be taught. It has a different connotation. All will look right depending on how one interprets them.

At that moment my eyes will be filled with sleep like the dense corn fields. At that time, my father would be yawning after a day's work.

Still, my mother would have unfinished household chores. She would feed straws to the cattle and would be making beetle leaves. She would sit with my elder aunt. My aunt would whisper something in her ears, and she would laugh.

Both behaved strangely. Sometimes they will quarrel and won't talk to each other for several days and some other times they will be so close that even water will not percolate between them.

My father and my elder uncle never paid attention to them when they fought or when they were close. Whenever there was a fight between them, elder aunty will say whatever she wishes; my mother would bring the basket and a small tin box from her room, throw it in the courtyard, and say: What did I hide in the box? Why don't you keep it? Who told you not to keep it? Even the walls in this house have ears.

My aunt would whimper and say: 'Ok, from today onwards, I am devoid of my eyes and ears, so if you get hurt, don't blame me. Henceforth if I utter a single word, you can keep a dog in my name.' My mother would mumble to herself while picking up the scattered things as she threw the box down. Those things include her silver bangles, pumpkin seeds, Kuehl container, an amulet made of octo-alloy, my father's childhood reed pen, and *Chaamara (kind of a hand fan made* from the tail hair of calves.

Both would become silent when my uncle would return from the oratorio. My uncle could apprehend that there was something wrong.

He would call me and ask: What happened? Why are all silent in the house?

I would reply: Aunt and mother fought.

He would laugh and ask: Who won?

I would give a smile and say: My mother.

Whenever there is a fight, my aunt and my mother would hide somewhere before my uncle's arrival.

Father would yell from the front yard and say: It's already 10 o'clock. that boy has not gone to school today. Where is that naughty fellow?

I would lie down on my uncle's lap and say: Uncle, I have been suffering from a fever since last night. I won't go to school today.

He would cuddle me and say: It's ok. Stay away from school today. Listening to him, my father would suddenly change his tune and say gently: Won't you go to school today?

My uncle would say: He has a high fever; let him not go to school today.

My father would say: He is a liar. He is trying to avoid going to school by giving lame excuses. He would again ask me: Are you going or not?

My uncle would say firmly: Let him not go today. He isn't well. What difference will it make if he doesn't go for a day?

Fettered, my father would walk away from there, and I would get up happily from my uncle's lap. He would say: Look! How I lied for you. I teach you not to lie, but I always lie for you.

I would look at my uncle's face, who had big eyes, and a huge head with a broader forehead with *tilak (an ornamental spot worn on the forehead chiefly by Hindus as a sectarian mark)*. Then I will start thinking I will go to school every day. You don't have to look at me. Okay?

My uncle would affectionately pull me towards him and say: I know… *Alekha* astrologer has checked your horoscope and told you - you will be highly educated and placed in a good job. You will be like *Madhu Babu*.

At that time, I didn't know much about *Madhu Babu*. I only knew that he wears a turban and rides on the back of a black horse, and children like us should follow his path when we grow up.

But I could never feel that my father paid more attention to the predictions made by my uncle. Instead, he became stricter, and to divert our attention toward studies, he bought a gramophone (which was a rare commodity in our area). The gramophone showed a picture of a dog sitting focused in front of a funnel resembling a *Dhatura* (Cascabel thevetin) flower. My uncle made me understand that it's a magical instrument that can even make a dog sing. We would listen to the song of *Nimai Charan Harichandan* on the gramophone. After listening to it, we didn't like the oratorio sung by my uncle. In the village, those who liked oratorio now ignored my uncle and wanted to listen to the song on the gramophone. They were captivated by the songs of *Nimai Harichandan* and slowly drifted away from my uncle. He was annoyed and dissatisfied by this.

We should have paid more attention to his annoyance, continued to listen to the gramophone, and ignored our studies. My father came to know about it. One day *Kuni* and I were listening to the gramophone in the morning, and suddenly, my father came. He yelled and said: You both are always listening to the music. When are you studying? In anger, he threw the gramophone into the courtyard, and my mother couldn't stop him from doing so.

The gramophone broke.

I felt like my heart also broke into pieces, along with

the gramophone. I started crying aloud. *Kuni* also cried. My mother was annoyed, and she refused to cook on that day. My father spoke rudely to her and said: If you give so much liberty to the children, then you must face the consequences, and he went outside angrily.

I took the broken gramophone to my study room. Both *Kuni* and I tried to repair it, but the gramophone was completely damaged. We couldn't fix it, and it made me cry once again.

In the evening, sitting on my uncle's lap and chewing *Mudhi* (Puffed Rice), I said: Uncle, the father broke the gramophone. Can't it be repaired?

He laughed and said: An instrument is an instrument. Does it have a body? If it gets spoilt, then it can never be repaired. It's good that it's broken. It was making a screeching sound, and I couldn't rest peacefully.

I could understand that my uncle was behind this episode. I knew that not only in our village but also in the nearby villages, my uncle didn't have any enemies, but two enemies crept up from nowhere- One of them was the 'dog on the gramophone. The other one was "*Nimai Charan Harichandan*" because slowly, people started listening to the gramophone rather than to my uncle's oratorio.

Deep within, I was very much annoyed with my uncle. My uncle spoke like a philosopher in a baritone. He said: This instrument will bewitch human beings and turn them into monsters. Humans will be the slave of it. This instrument will feed humans, make them sleep, and sing for them. It will make all human beings torpid.

I didn't pay any heed to what my uncle said. Instead, if an instrument could do all these things, then it would be better. Suddenly I will recall what my father said. He said: Whatever uncle is saying isn't true. I would again feel like crying. Butonuncle will be singing *Malika (A religious text about the future)* with a lot of passion on a high note.

My house is in Chhatia village…

It is on the east side of Amaravati, Oh! Lily Flower!

Creating havoc,

All will lose their mind.

The elf will engulf all, Oh! Lily Flower!

It will be over in the blink of the eyes

You terrified devotees…

Your ears will long for the name of God, Oh! Lily Flower!

He will be the savior and protect all devotees….

I would be falling asleep and trying to keep them open.

Isaw my father and a man having tea and puffed rice together. He was smiling but as soon as my father became grave, he looked at his stony face and gave a deadpan stare. My mother and aunt were listening to their conversation by stealth.

I asked my mother: Who is this man?

My mother said: He recently joined the village school as a teacher. His name is *Laxmidhar*, Sir.

My aunt said: Now you will study under him.

I said: I will never study.

My aunt said: What can't be done at a young age? Can that be done in old age?

I began my studies. I will sit and look at the books in *Laxmidhar* Sir's house before and after my school hours. I was confident that I would get beaten while studying. *Laxmidhar* Sir was cruel like my father, but his wife was lovable. She liked me and fed me with a variety of pancakes. She was fair and adored her forehead with a spot of vermilion. Sometimes *Laxmidhar* Sir would beat her, and I didn't like it. I thought of hitting *Laxmidhar sir a few times*, Sir, but I couldn't because he also loved me.

Laxmidhar Sir had a niece who was studying along with me. Both of us were studying together and, in our free time, ran after the dragonfly.

My mother loved both of us. By the time we were in school, my elder brother was studying in a high school ten miles away from our house. My elder brother sat at his study table at night and drew pictures. He drew different types of flowers and colored them and wrote something. When I asked him about it, he said: We are taught all these things in school.

We are not taught something like this. How much time it takes to fill a tank and how much time it takes to empty a tank? How much time it will take to fill the tank? If A, B, and C can do a piece of work in seven days, A, D, and E can finish it in 3 days. If D, E, and F work together, how many days will they finish the work? Yuck, what type of calculation is this? More than these calculations *Laxmidhar* Sir and his cane are dreadful. I always remembered my brother's colorful pictures when these calculations were taught. Those were so colorful and interesting. I felt as if I am like a monkey trying to climb a pole. The more I try to climb, I slip down.

Laxmidhar Sir said: This boy can never study.

I liked what he said as I wanted sir to convey this message to my father so I wouldn't learn.

I had lost many things due to these studies. I always felt that I couldn't do many things because I went to school and studied. I couldn't go to the nearby forest at the top of the hill in search of the thorny berries, couldn't pluck mangoes and plums, couldn't play with my friend *Punia. Nidhia and Bhikari are* on the old banyan tree and swing like a monkey. All these areas were forbidden for me after the arrival of *Laxmidhar* Sir.

I had an ardent desire to get rid of studying, but one

fine day, my father came to *Laxmidhar* sir's house and said: Sir, beat this boy as much as you can. If you can't beat him, then let me know. If he dies because of your beatings, it doesn't matter because it's better not to have a son than to have a dumb one. My eyes were filled with tears when I heard such harsh words. I went and told my mother. My mother supported my father and said: Whatever your father has said is for your well-being.

My aunt said: If you don't study properly, then like *Nidhia*, the cattle herder, you will also herd the cattle or work in the fields. If you learn properly, you can become an officer and ride a car.

My uncle, while tying his hair with a marigold flower, said: Listen, son! Knowledge is the gist. Rest others have no meaning. There is a saying that an educated scheduled caste boy can also sing songs if he is educated. Knowledge is the route. Everyone must get educated. I could realize that no one supports me in this house, and there is a planned conspiracy going against me. I felt as if my father, mother, uncle, and aunt are my enemies. Can I ever get rid of them?

At that time, my maternal grandfather came to our house. He brought with him some sweetmeats and mango jelly candies, which were made by my grandmother.

Whenever my grandfather came, he always wanted me to be with him. He would tell me stories and teach me Odia literary composition genres (*Chhanda, Champu, Odishi*). As long as my grandfather is at home, there won't be many restrictions on me. My grandfather narrated many stories, but my elder brother said my grandfather was a brag. He said that my grandfather's name is not included in the list of freedom fighters, which is there in his history book.

But I never doubted what my grandfather says. Instead, I thought that my brother is lying.

My grandfather stayed in our house for a week. He wanted to take me along with him for a few days. My father could never say 'No' to my grandfather. Still, he was annoyed and said to my mother: I think the boy will become an illiterate fool, and all of you will be responsible for it.

My mother said: Why are you telling me all these things? Why don't you say it to him?

My father could never say anything to my grandfather. I went to my maternal uncle's place with my grandfather to get rid of the conspiracy of the people in our house and *Laxmidhar* sir.

After getting down from the bus and walking through the fields, there is a runnel. After crossing the runnel is my maternal uncle's village.

There were no restrictions in my grandfather's house. No one was there to say anything, even if I roamed around. There was always good food, and my maternal grandmother was pleased to see me. *Sapani*, my maternal uncle, was directing a play for a group of lazybones in the school building. He would take me to the school building in the evening, and as the nephew of the *Ustad* (Master), his followers would gift me fried groundnuts, nuts, etc.

I would completely forget about my house being there in my maternal grandfather's house. One day, suddenly, my father would arrive at my grandfather's house and ask me: Did you forget about your studies?

I nodded my head and said: Of course, I remember.

My father would ask: I have two hands. Can you translate this into English?

I would take a bite and say: I have two handez.

My father would get angry and say: Come home with me, then I will let you know. I will ensure that you have a bandage on your hadez…

My father can't beat me in front of my grandfather, so he purred like a *Singi* (Fossil cat) fish.

Despite my reluctance, I had to return with my father leaving behind the lustrous green environment, the runnel banks adorned with *Ketaki* (screw pine) flowers and *Deepadandi* (the central wood log) of the green village pond.

As soon as I reached home, my uncle would say: Oh! You remembered us after a long time, isn't it?

Kuni will say: Brother, you left the village, and after that, there was a circus party in our village for fifteen days. In the circus, a white bear was riding a bicycle.

I regretted it as I couldn't see the circus. My mother would ask me only about my grandmother, grandfather, uncle, and aunt.

I won't reply and sit quietly.

By the time I started studying in a college in the city, my uncle had already grown old. Dousing kerosene, his only daughter *Sakhi's* sister was burnt by her in-laws, and after that incident, my uncle stopped conversing with others. Whenever I return to the village from the city, he won't speak to me much. I was staying in the hostel, and my father visited me once or twice a month. Once a month, I would drop a letter to my father conveying that- there is a lot of expenditure this month as I bought many books, there is a hike in the college dues, so please send me some more money. Upon receiving the letter, Father would visit the hostel with the cash, sweets, and pancakes my mother had prepared, and the village deity's vermillion and sacred thread.

Gangadhar was my roommate. My father got along well with him. *Ganga* and my father sit together and talk for a long time. *Gangadhar* is entirely learned. He can deliberate on Hindu scriptures, and folk poetry and sing *Bhagavat* with many emotions. When my father listens to his song, he becomes emotional. In a musical tone, with all devotion he sings, *the idols of Krishna... oh Lord, what matters is chanting of your name....*

My father's eyes also get filled with tears. *Ganga* also sings with rapt attention, with his eyes filled with tears. He wipes his tears and tells my father: You may think it's a lie, but it's a truth for me. Fifteen days before, I dreamt of

Lord Jagannath waking me up from my sleep and saying, *Gangadhar-* wake up. When I woke up, I saw that the photo that is hanging on the wall nw was on my bed. I was laughing to myself, listening to *Gangadhar*. I know that *Gangadhar* is a religious addict, but I couldn't say anything because of my father. I could see my father becoming emotional listening to *Gangadhar*.

My father would say: Son, you are blessed. Let it be in a dream or reality; you could see God. Saying this, my father would look at me, and I could infer what he intended to convey from his looks. He might say: you stay in the same room, but only one can see God. What about you? You unlucky fellow!

I couldn't look at my father's eyes. I look down and read D.H Lawrence.

After speaking to *Ganga,* my father would narrate all the incidents in the village to me. He would say: How the *Ravi* crop was spoiled due to insects and how the government wasn't supplying water in the canal. After becoming a *moharir,* How *Sabaraa Sahoo*'s son divided the village into two. How a Monocled Cobra confronted *Bidia Jena's* son for two hours.

My father would speak to us till late at night but would wake up early and prepare to return to the village. *Ganga* would say: Uncle, please stay for one more day. My father would laugh and say: I want to stay with you for a fortnight, but what can be done? The pond in the backyard needs to be cleaned; it's time to yield the crops; four bunches of bananas are almost ready to rip, and if the thieves come to know about it, they will steal. The cattle suffered from dysentery, so I must call the veterinary doctor.

My father would leave the hostel at dawn. *Ganga* and I would go to the bus stand to drop him off. While boarding the bus, Father would say: Come to the village during your holidays. Your elder aunty has slowed down. She is remembering you and wants to meet you. I tried to console her saying he has a lot to read, I don't know whether he can make it or not. Still, you try to come. I would nod my head and say 'Yes'.

The bus would leave, and we will return once fathers elbow and glasses become invisible. '

I would remember my aunt and feel sad, and the day would pass gloomily. *Ganga* would ask me the reason for my sadness. I would say: I am thinking about my aunt. Do you know *Ganga*, my aunt, loves me a lot?

Ganga would say: It's better if you go to the village tomorrow. Go and meet your aunt and return the next day.

I couldn't go to the village the next day because the next day I was supposed to go for a picnic with *Nita Mishra* to *Harishankar*. I told *Ganga:* I am going to my village but went for a picnic. In the vehicle, *Nita Mishra* was sitting next to me. Her beautiful, naughty, and talkative friend *Arunaa* was sitting in the front seat. She mocked us a few times. *Nita Mishra* was sleeping, leaning on my shoulder. She was saying: Please, don't deprive me of the good luck of sleeping on your shoulders forever. I was grateful to *Nita Mishra* as my first fiancée, but (maybe) I was like her last lover.

In between, *Nita Mishra* narrated the story about her pet cat and its mischief for almost two hours. I told you: Thailand has a type of cat that changes its color every season. *Nita Mishra* was astonished, and she asked: Is it true?

I remembered my mother and aunt. When I was in grade five, we had two cats in our house. They had some names and were fed rice, fish, and *chapattis*. Sometimes they ate with my aunt. By the time I was in High School, their number grew to almost ten or twelve; by the time I was in college, they grew to twenty or more. My aunt had named each one of them, and they would come to her once she calls out their names. One of the cats jumped on my study table and spilled the ink bottle. I was angry and threw a paperweight at him, and it died.

My aunt took the dead cat in her arms and cried, calling: *Oh My Sania'*. At that time, I learned that the cat's name was *Sania.*

It is said that killing a cat brings misfortune, so salt equal to the cat's weight was thrown in the well, a Brahmin was fed, and a blanket was donated. After that incident, my aunt warned me that I should never kill a cat as they are related to the goddess Lakshmi.

I laughed. *Nita Mishra* asked: Why did you laugh?

I said: I remembered the story of a cat, but I get irritated with cats.

Nita Mishra asked: Why?

I said: Someone has indeed said that a cat should die after five years and a woman at twenty; otherwise, they turn selfish.

Aruna laughed and asked: Is it true or a joke?

I laughed and said: Are all jokes lies?

After visiting the waterfall and mountain and picnicking in *Harishankar*, we returned, and by that time, *Aruna* was too tired. *Nita Mishra* put her head on my shoulder and was humming a song. I could sniff the fragrance of her unkempt hair and felt romantic. I was enchanted by the scent of her body. *Nita Mishra* held me tightly and said: 'I love you'. I was losing track of the fragrance of *Nita Mishra.*

I reached the hostel near dawn. *Ganga* was plucking flowers after completing his daily chores. He looked at me seriously and didn't talk to me.

I entered the room, changed my clothes, and slept for some time. *Ganga* came to the room and started chanting the prayer … *Deity of Krishna is God…* After some time, he lit the stove, prepared tea with the milk powder, offered me a cup, and said: You have not gone to the village?

I nodded and said 'No'. I felt as if *Ganga* is my guardian.

Ganga became serious and asked me: Why did you lie about visiting the village? It's Ok. Get ready and go to the village immediately, yesterday I got the news that your aunt is seriously ill. I have *Ganga* Water and *Nirmalya* (*sacred dried rice from the Jagannath temple*) with me. You can take that along with you.

I got ready, and *Ganga* dropped me in his cycle at the bus stand. He said: If your aunt is extremely unwell, don't return. I will take care of the attendance.

By the time I reached my village, it was almost noon. My uncle was sitting on the porch without any expression. My father sat stunned, and my younger uncle was arranging the wood. I sat down near my uncle. His eyes were closed, and he was engrossed in deep thought. He gave a cold glance and said: Go inside the house. Your aunt remembered you a lot yesterday but can't recognize anyone today.

A bunch of thick sadness choked my throat. I entered the house. My aunt was sleeping; surrounded by mother, younger aunty, relatives, and the ladies from the neighborhood. My mother was sobbing. I sat near my aunt and called her: Aunt …. Aunt… She neither opened her eyes nor responded. Tears rolled down my eyes. I could hear her noisy breath. I felt like crying a lot. The cough also choked me.

My mother shook my aunt and called: Sister… sister! Look, your son is calling you.

Once my mother called her, an aunt made her mouth move a bit. Mother told me to make her drink the sacred water from the temple kept in a glass. I took a spoon and made her drink the holy water and, along with that, made her drink the *Ganga* water that *Gangadhar* had given me. My aunt gulped the water as if she was very thirsty. She opened her eyes and looked at me. Maybe she couldn't recognize me.

I was in tears; left the place to enter my study room. I only used the study room for a few years. My brother, after taking up a job in Delhi, never visited the house, so the room wasn't in use. The books in the room needed to be appropriately kept. When I used to study in the room, my aunt would call me repeatedly and say: Oh! Why don't you go and have your food? Her responsibility was to take care of the food for the entire family. She took care of each one's likes and dislikes.

Now, she is sleeping, non-responsive; lying down as if she is dead. Human life is so unpredictable. The deity of so many people, so many fights and misunderstandings; so much of humanity and love was slowly turning into a stone… darkness pervaded my eyes.

Oh God! I hold my palm tightly against my eyes and cried bitterly.

My aunt died around the evening.

My mother lost her voice due to crying. The ladies from the neighborhood also cried and tried to console her. My mother pushed their hands and wept: Where did you go leaving me behind—oh my sister… did you move away from this straw house .. oh, my sister…

My uncle was sitting quietly without any expression like a rock. His eyes were dangling like glasses. *Maala bhai* (the villagers who lift the dead bodies) and my father lifted the dead body to the cremation ground.

Since my elder brother wasn't available, so I had to perform the last rites. My aunt perished under the log fire. I stayed in the village for eleven days, but my mother didn't speak a word to me. She continued to remember my aunt. My father appeared to be a very different person. There was utter silence in the house. I felt as if in my house, no one knows the other person.

I was restless and wanted to go back to the hostel. I was about to leave on the twelfth day when my mother asked: Are you leaving today?

I nodded my head in affirmation.

Mother's remorseful voice: why can't you stay a few more days?

My father said: What will he do here? Let him go as he hasn't attended the classes for almost twelve days.

I started for the hostel. I bowed down before the uncle and said: I am leaving. His eyes roved impatiently as if searching for something, and then they became still. I left the village and walked towards the bus stand. On the way, I had to cross the cremation ground, where I could see a dead body burning, and a smoke ring rising towards the sky. On the pathways of the fields, the dewdrops over unknown, white grass flowers, still shining in the sunlight. For some unknown reason, I felt like weeping. It felt as if I took a very long time to comprehend my parents, aunty, the river, and my village or maybe I won't understand them for the whole of my life.

When I reached the hostel, I saw that *Ganga* was sad. Usually, he is low when he is alone. but on that day, I felt he was a lonelier despairing pair. Tired, heartbroken,

From the depth of silence, *Ganga* asked: Were all the rites appropriately performed? I thought he is not my roommate and spoke as if he is a responsible person like my father and uncle. I embraced *Ganga* and cried like a small child.

Holding Ganga hard, like a small child, I wept. Like an elderly person, *Ganga* patted my back and said: You are born as a mortal, why should you fear death?

I am aware that *Ganga* never goes to his village during holidays. He has a stepmother and an uncle in the village. Sometimes he remembers his parents and feels sad, but he cannot recall what his parents looked like because he had lost them in his early days. During the vacation, he stays alone in the hostel. He has his food at Sahu Hotel when the hostel mess is closed during holidays. He never eats non-vegetarian and never lies.

After a while, *Ganga* said: A letter in your name came almost four days back.

I wiped my tears and opened the letter. The letter was from *Nita Mishra*. She wrote that she remembered me, cried, and recollected all her memories. Through the letter, she tried to stir her love and pain.

I left the hostel to meet *Nita Mishra.* I was feeling a little better after reading the letter. I tried to forget the expressionless face of my aunt and tried to recollect the beautiful look of *Nita Mishra.*

Ganga saw me leaving the room and asked: Where are you going?

I said: I am going to meet *Nita Mishra.*

Ganga didn't say anything.

Nita Mishra was absent from the hostel. Her naughty friend *Aruna* said that she had gone outside with *Ananta bhai* to watch a movie and that he is a distant relative of *Nita* and is studying Engineering in Mumbai. I couldn't ask her anything more.

Aruna said: What should I inform *Nita?*

I said: No, nothing as such. You can tell her that I have come to meet her and left the place.

I couldn't get proper sleep the whole day and night; was restless and felt like crying. I felt as if I am a loser. I am losing things one by one, and one day, I will be left with nothing.

I saw my aunt in the dream. I could see her among the ghosts who looked like the jokers with red and blue masks. She was weeping and sad. I could see her for some time, and then she vanished like dark smoke. Then *Nita Mishra arrived* in white attire like a fairy. She was singing a melodious song and I don't know when the song metamorphosed into the bellowing of my aunt.

There was some night left when I woke up. *Ganga was* sitting near the table, and the lights were still switched on. I could never sleep when the lights are switched on, but I felt comfortable with the glowing light. The fear also receded a bit.

I asked *Ganga:* Why didn't you sleep? He looked at me. His eyes were red. Maybe he was probably crying.

I asked him: What happened?

Ganga said with teary eyes: I was reading *Shakuntala. Shakuntala* was the adopted daughter of Saint *Kanva.* On her separation, Saint *Kanva* said: *Jasyadatya Shakuntalati eti hrudayam spasm mutkanthya (After that the heart stopped beating)* .... Why a saint is not able to bear this separation?

Had it been some other day, I would joke with *Ganga* and whisper *Ganga* from narrating it but on that, I had some comfort in his words. It was new and being curious, I asked: then what next?

Then *Ganga* didn't say much. He cried. I have never seen *Ganga* crying this way. I took him by my side but was unable to make him understand. Both of us embraced each other and cried for a long time like two helpless, orphan brothers of the world.

The next day I met *Nita Mishra* in the college. I pretended as if I didn't see her. She came near me and said: Are you annoyed?

I said: 'No'.

Nita held my hand and said: I am not in the mood to attend the class.

I asked her: Who is *Ananta*? *Nita Mishra* laughed and said: Oh! Is that the reason for your anger? He is my brother, not my fiancée. You are my fiancée, you and only you.

After listening to *Nita Mishra,* my heart melted. She took my hand in her sweaty hand and asked: Don't you trust me?

I smiled and thought that I was not alone in this world. I have *Nita Mishra* with me; her lap is a haven for me.

Nita Mishra smiled. She looks beautiful when she smiles. She said: As I love you, I have stopped thinking about my caste, family background, and reputation. I don't know if my family will ever accept you, but I know how difficult it is to live without you. May God not give the sorrow from being away from the beloved, even to the worst enemy.

I became sad listening to what *Nita Mishra* said. *Nita Mishra* continued by saying: Do you know my father isn't so mean in this matter because he also had a love marriage? My mother won't complain much, but my grandfather is a conservative Brahmin, so he mightn't accept you. He may commit suicide, but I can't leave you. I can't.

I lovingly touched the mane of *Nita Mishra* and said: We will live together, die together,r and to get you is one of the biggest challenges in my life. If I don't get you….

Nita Mishra's eyes were filled with tears.

So also, mine!.

When I returned to the hostel, I saw my father sitting there. He was preparing black tea with ginger for my father. *Ganga* wasn't sad anymore.

I touched my father's feet. I never thought that he would come. He said: I reached here just an hour back. Where did you go? I said: I had my classes.

Ganga served tea and then went to the shop to get a beetle. I looked at my father keenly. He had lost a lot of weight. He didn't look happy and contented. He looked as if he had lost his confidence. He seemed to be broken.

I suspected something serious had happened as my father came without any information. What has happened? Is there anyone who is sick at home?

My father could read my mind. He said: Why are you worried? Everything is fine. After your aunt expired, there is a void in life. I am not feeling good. I remembered you and your mother insisted me to come and meet you. Your elder brother didn't turn up. Your aunt wanted to meet him, but she couldn't, and after her demise, your uncle is not taking food properly. He has become lean and thin. He told me yesterday evening to inform you to come and meet him.

He cried and said: Don't you ever remember your uncle? That is why I came. He again said: Please visit your uncle if you don't have classes.

Father didn't eat anything at dinner and said his stomach was upset. After my aunt expired, my father stopped taking food properly. He looked aged now with wrinkles on his face. But was Aunt so close to my father? As far as I remember, they don't speak much with each other. I have often noticed that when my uncle and father go to some other place for work and are late home, my mother becomes restless. She walks up and down the courtyard, and my aunt sits and waits for them near the front door. For me, it's time to enjoy it as both aren't present. I play on the swing and sometimes go to *Pandia* mango grove, pluck mangoes, and eat. The children assemble in our courtyard in the evening, and the game begins. We play various games.

Gilli… Gilli…Gundi,

Gilli…. Gilli …. Gundi,

Go and get the money from your mother.

Mother said there was no money.

 How will you get the sweet?

Threw them into the dung pit….

The crow took me away to my maternal uncle's home.

Maternal uncle's wife asked who he is…

Let me clean it and take home.

Let me give you a fistful of milk and rice.

And let me slip him below the storehouse…

The children would be shouting in the courtyard. My aunt would say: Why are you going round and round like a swirl? Your head will start reeling. Move slowly.

My mother would say: hey, Is it not time for you to study? Let your father come. If I don't tell him, then I am not the daughter of *Manguli Swain*… Will you go and study or not?

I don't care for my mother's single word. I would lightly take my mother's words and reply: Go and tell Father. What can he do? I will play, play, and play.

I knew well that my mother would never say this to my father. While having food if my father asks: Did he study properly today? Before I could reply, my aunt would say: He lit the lantern in the evening and was sitting with his books. My father would say gravely,' Ok,' and then look at me. I would be scared that my father would come to know that I didn't study. I would take a deep breath and think: How will Father come to know? I would feel relieved. Thank you, aunt, thank you.

Sometimes if I am caught by my father while playing, then it would be a bad day for me. He will hold my ear, pull me from there, and make me stand on one leg. He would say: Touch your nose on the ground and kneel keeping a pebble below your knees. This would continue for almost two hours or till I cry. I would be feeling desperate to cry; fluid from the running nose mixed with tears would flow into my mouth. Mother, without uttering a word, would be preoccupied inside the kitchen.

Then she will come out and speak to my father: I must prepare dal. Go and get it from the shop.

My father would say: It's not necessary to prepare dal. Let me settle the matter with the by first.

My mother knows very well about my father's anger. She will remain quiet. My aunt would come and say: He wasn't well yesterday. He had a fever. Why did you make him stand in this hot Sun for so long?

My father would say: You all are doctors in this house. I know how to bring down his fever. In this house, there are only two children. The elder one is already there in high school, and this boy only wants to play with the other worthless boys in the village near the pond and the mango grove.

He will look at me and say: You will never study as you don't want to. From tomorrow onwards, you will go along with the son of *Nidhia Behera,* rear the cattle, and take them to the field for grazing. Is that fine?

I would feel happy and think it would be good if my father would send me to take the cattle for grazing. It will be fun to climb the mountains, pluck berries from the thorny bushes, climb the tree, sit on its branches, and play the flute. But my condition is worse than *Nidhia Behera's* sons. I would say to myself: Father! Please relieve me from the burden of my studies.

My father would come near me, twitch my ear and say: What happened? Why can't you utter a single word now? You are standing like an innocent child, but create chaos when you step outside the house.

He will say: I will teach you a lesson today and take out a stock prod. By looking at it, I would start praying to all the gods and goddesses to help me so that my father won't hit me with the stock pod. In the meantime, my father would hear my uncle's voice, hide the stock pod, and leave the house quietly through the backyard door. My uncle would enter the house and ask for some water.

He would come near me as I stood on one leg in the hot Sun. He would wipe my sweat with his towel, lift me and shout: You are torturing the child by making him stand in this hot sun. I would cry loudly, listening to my uncle, and my mother and aunt would look at each other's faces and smile. I would sob and say: Uncle, Father would have killed me if you wouldn't come.

My mother and aunt never restricted my father from punishing me, so I will teach them a lesson.

My uncle would touch my hair gently and say: How could your father dare to beat you? Let him come. I will teach him a lesson. Is it the way to discipline a child? If a child goes astray, then the mother must practice strict regimentation. Has a father ever practiced severe regimentation to reform a child? Whenever Lord Krishna played mischief, his mother, *Yashoda*, tried to improve him, and his father, *Nanda*, never interfered.

When I woke up, the door was open, and my father was sitting on a chair. He was looking outside. Now a day's, my father doesn't interfere with my study matter. I am more educated than my father now. My father completed his matric at that time. He left his job and opened a school in the village. My grandmother scolded my father until her death as he used the bricks to keep constructing our house and the school.

She would say: You gave the bricks marked for your own house to others, and now, other than you, who will stay in this broken house?

Am I more erudite than my father, who didn't accept any honorarium and taught in the school because he wanted to be free? He recited the poems of the poets like national poets *Birakishore* and *Banchanidhi* and worked for the country's freedom. He went from door to door and asked for alms. He never told a lie, was never scared of anyone, and taught me about the truth and reality. He will always advise me to save wealth and righteousness. Can I ever be sapient like him?

My father, who was resilient and gritty, handled the situation with all his strength, but now he is sitting silently. Didn't he sleep properly at night? What is he thinking?

I strolled towards my father and stood beside him.

My father asked: Didn't you sleep? I couldn't give a reply and stood there silently.

We looked at each other's faces silently. For the first time, I looked at his face directly. There is no change in his facial features. I felt as if I was seeing him for the first time.

My father's face has not changed a bit at all. The same eyes, the same elevated forehead, and the same face matured with experience. I felt as if I am seeing him for the first time. I never realized that there was so much compassion in his eyes. Was my father trying to hide his sorrows for so many years, or is it necessary to hide the grief when you become a father?

Father said: I will leave tomorrow. If you find time, then make a trip to the village.

Like every time, Father was ready to go early in the morning because getting a bus to our village is a challenge- he won't get a bus if he misses the first one. My father always took the bus when he came to visit me or left for the village. He was punctual.

This time, I made my father sit on the bicycle and dropped him at the bus stand. While alighting the bus, he said: Whenever you go to the village, purchase the *Achyutananda Malika* book for your uncle. He has told me a few times about it, but I forgot to mention it in the past. He is reading the *Gupta Gita* daily, which you had earlier given him.

The bus left. I came back to the hostel. During his visit, my father only spoke a little with *Ganga*. *Ganga* asked me: What happened to your father? He didn't talk to me appropriately.

I replied: My uncle isn't well, so my father is a little upset. I must go to the village.

Ganga said: I also want to visit and see your uncle, but I must study and complete the course. I felt lonely and told *Ganga*: Let's visit my village together. Let's go tomorrow, and we will be back in two days. I, along with *Ganga*, left for the village the very next day.

Instead of being silent, my uncle had turned talkative. He was overwhelmed. He looked at me and said: Oh! After so many days, you remembered this old man, right? He was also happy to meet *Ganga*.

I said: Uncle, *Ganga* has a vast knowledge of sacred scriptures. My uncle smiled and said: I could make out by looking at him that he was knowledgeable. But son! Do you know anything about theology? You need to know about it to be knowledgeable. Unless you have a depth of understanding of the same, you will never get into real education!

My mother told us to have our food. My uncle said: We will discuss theology at night. I don't like to discuss theology, but *Ganga* has a lot of interest in it. He said: Ok, we will discuss it.

We sat in the courtyard at night. The air was filled with the sweet fragrance of mogra flower at night. I was sitting along with *Ganga*. I had a thought in my mind to reveal *Nita Mishra to Ganga.*, but then my uncle came. He created a betel paste in the betel hammer and said: Why is theology not included in your curriculum? It's the most critical part of education. Your education and knowledge are only complete if you know about it. Right from my childhood, I have found my uncle quite mysterious. He gives the example of religious beliefs and theory to sort out the problems in the village, but today, he sounded different. I felt as if it was not my uncle but someone else spoke. His voice was heavy and choked with phlegm. He cleared his throat and sang:

It is said…

it's the foible of the womb…

the sin of the past life.

The body will turn into ashes…

Pray to purify the heart and

make us abide in him forever,

you will complete the ride

with purity and righteousness.

Ganga's eyes were filled with tears. My uncle was reciting in his style and explaining the hymn's meaning. : Gentlemen…. Did you understand? The man of conscience is explaining the deeper thoughts. Dear percipience, pray to the Almighty. If your body is like a chariot, the almighty is the charioteer.

My uncle and *Ganga* were discussing deep into the night. Compared to previous instances, he was lesser in mute mode. He laughed, spoke, and sang songs. I was surprised as I saw a change in his behavior. He took the book on the future (*Bhabishya Maalika)* in his hand, touched it on his forehead, and read it loudly.

Ganga and I returned to the hostel the very next day. When we were about to leave, my uncle said: If possible, get me a *Kalki Purna* (The holy scripture on *Kalki*- the tenth incarnation of Vishnu). When I reached the hostel, I saw *Nita Mishra* drying her wet hair in the sun. She reached me and said: You weren't there for two days and something big had happened.

I was curious and asked: What had happened?

Nita said: My father has fixed my marriage with a Junior Engineer. He and his friend came to the hostel to meet me.

I couldn't utter a word. I asked: What is your opinion about the proposal?

Nita Mishra cried and said: I know what I say will hurt you, but I belong to a Brahmin family. We are taught not to defy the decision taken by the elders in the family. It is not a part of our family culture. I don't know what to do. Sometimes I think of confronting the age-old tradition, but I become helpless whenever I look at my father. My father has asked me to come home, and I have to go tomorrow.

I was disappointed and asked her: What should I do next?

Nita Mishra said: Look, If I come back from my

home, then I am yours, and if I don't come back, then it's apparent that I got married. I beg you to forget me once I get married. Please discard all the letters and photos of mine and …..

-Are you saying to forget you? I can understand. I told this to her and went back to the hostel. My eyes were filled with tears, and I didn't attend my classes. I cried for a long time and then took out the letters and photos of *Nita Mishra.* I glanced for once and then burnt those.

Along with the letters and the photos, there was an end to the story of my first love, my sentiments, and my tribal heartbeats. As those got burnt, I felt a little insouciant and tried to erase the memories of *Nita Mishra.* But is it possible to forget the first love and its sentiments so quickly? Instead, my throat was choked, and my sensitivity and affectivity defeated me. I was shattered.

Ganga came back to the hostel room after attending his classes. He was surprised to see me on the bed and asked: Why didn't you attend the lessons today?

I was silent. He didn't ask me anything further and walked away from there. He went and sat on his bed, closed his eyes, and was engrossed in his thoughts.

I didn't say anything to *Ganga* about *Nita Mishra* because I knew that if I told him, he would lecture me on Vaishnav philosophy and love, or he would give me an example of platonic love and tell me that love is inspired by nobler pursuits. A pure soul is the co-carrier of pure love. If I had told *Ganga* about my relationship and feelings beforehand, he would have shown me a way out of this dystopia. I would have reconciled, and my mood would have been alleviated, but I could never pour out my heart to *Ganga*. Instead, I endured the twinge within. The metamorphosis began. The tender-hearted, intelligent life form within me eventually assumed the form of vices of jealousy, sufferance, and hatred.

After a long time, I saw my aunt in my dream who from the time I could recall, never removed her veil; she stood with her hair open and, without the veil, looked like a witch. She couldn't recognize me. She looked savage and showed raw hunger. After a while, she turned into a ball of soft cotton, then into a cloud parcel, then a bird, and finally mingled in the thin air.

I couldn't sleep for the rest of the night. I was on edge and felt lonely. I left my bed, opened the door, and peeped outside. In the deemed moonlight, the Croton plants in the garden stood silently like my uncle. Usually, whenever there is any problem in the village, my uncle stands there silently, and all the conflicts come to an end immediately as if he is an indomitable mountain.

It was a bit cold outside, and I felt better and lighter. The memories of *Nita Mishra* didn't engulf me anymore. I tried to console myself and thought: Let *Nita Mishra* leave my life. What is her entity in my life? I have my village; my father; my uncle; my mother; my courtyard with *Tulsi* plant> There is a perennial fragrance of mogra flower. They are still alive in my memoir. They flourish in my sentience. With the fragrance, entrenched are the memories of my childhood days and youth. I was intrigued by the vivid memories of my childhood and the sweet scent of mogra, which lingered and tried to dismiss the inklings of *Nita Mishra*.

Nita Mishra got married and didn't return to the hostel. I received her wedding invitation. She forgot me and led a happy and contented life with her husband.

I also forgot *Nita Mishra* and concentrated on my studies. Nita Mishra slowly became a memory and from memory turned into darkness.

I finished my examination and returned to my village, and *Ganga* left the hostel. *Ganga* became sentimental while leaving the hostel. He had swollen eyes while leaving the hostel. I knew he was a very sentimental kid and that *Ganga* couldn't pursue his studies as his uncle and stepmother would never allow him to study further. Slowly *Ganga* will look older than his age, either sitting at home or searching for a job.

At home, I didn't feel happy for quite some time as I was nostalgic. I remembered my good old days in the hostel, the chaos, the sad face of *Ganga,* and the hoodwink of *Nita Mishra,* I would have never felt so desolate if *Nita Mishra* had been with me. I felt as if love is like anesthesia that controls the mind and keeps a person away from too much sadness and pain.

Am I right?

I asked the question to myself and gave a reply to myself: Ah! Um! Let it be love, a love of delusion, but if it could have drawn breath.

I was still thinking with so much devotion about *Nita Mishra,* but does she remember me? Would she be remembering me while looking at the moon in the sky at night or a dove couple on the street? Would she be reading my letters? She might have burnt all the photos and the letters.

In a true sense, I felt lonely in the village. My childhood friends didn't behave like how they behaved before. The village club room had a lot of chaos, politics, and infightings. People were more interested in watching videos, gossip, politics, and controversy. One of my friends close to the MLA had become a hooligan and was troubling people, but the village elders couldn't tell him anything. So I became lonely in the village.

My uncle seemed much older than his age and spent most of his time sleeping. He wasn't able to walk properly; he appeared dull and lifeless with swollen legs. He was no more handsome than before, as he had lost his curly hair; he appeared bald; but the forehead always had a glowing sectarian mark. Despite being old, he will wake up early in the morning, bathe in the river, and pray to Lord Surya. He wasn't as talkative as before and remained silent most of the time. Our house was no noisier. Instead, day by day, the silence had spread its wings in the house with a feeling of weeping all around. I was preparing for my interview in the evening and spending the whole day at the village market. My mother who was earlier was cheerful, but she became silent after my elder brother got married and settled down in Delhi. I was going crazy with the silence, inattentiveness, and restlessness around me.

At night, while having dinner, my father asked: Are you looking for a job?

I replied: I have appeared for the competitive examinations but was unsuccessful in getting one as they are asking for donations in most places.

My father said: Write a letter to your brother. He may be able to help you.

I didn't reply to anything. I knew my elder brother didn't have time to listen to all these. He is busy with his LIC, stock exchange. He has been selfish right from childhood. He never allowed anyone to touch his books, dresses, or anything that belonged to him.

At that time, my father used to say: Look! How responsible is your elder brother? Look at yourself. Are you responsible? You are a wretch.

I looked straight into my father's face and said: I will get a job according to my efforts and won't take anyone's help.

Maybe my father felt happy. What was he expecting from me? I knew my father wasn't pleased with my elder brother because of his callous attitude toward the family. When my aunt expired, my brother didn't come for her last rituals.

I heard my father angrily saying to my mother, 'I disown my elder son.' I didn't like my brother and sister-in-law. They were materialistic. My brother was like that from childhood, so I disagreed with others when they said that my brother's attitude had changed after marriage as he listened to his wife. My mother longed for my brother. When we all sat together for dinner, she remembered my brother and became sentimental.

In between, my brother and sister-in-law visited the village. My father didn't speak to him though he felt restless for my brother. My brother also didn't speak to my father out of fear. He talked to me regarding my job. My sister-in-law didn't know Odia, and I was ashamed of speaking to her in Hindi at home.

My mother hugged my sister-in-law, cried, and said:

Where were you all for these days? Three people in this house were remembering you. Do you remember us? Tell me, who else is there for us other than you?

My sister-in-law couldn't understand what my mother was speaking. She smiled. My mother prepared lentils, boiled mixed vegetables, and other Odia delicacies. She had her food and appreciated the cooking by saying: beautiful, excellent.

While having lunch, my brother and sister-in-law discussed purchasing a plot in Delhi. They were speaking in Hindi, so my mother couldn't understand anything and asked them a few questions in between. She was insisting to have all varieties of food prepared for them. My brother and sister-in-law didn't notice her words as they seriously discussed the plot.

It was for the first time that my father didn't have lunch with us. I felt like we were strangers, sitting in a hotel and having our food.

My brother and sister-in-law stayed for a few days and left for Delhi. While returning, my mother asked: When will you revisit us? My brother looked at her and smiled. My uncle blessed both and said: wherever you stay, be happy and leave peacefully.

I accompanied them to the station, but at that time, my father wasn't present in the house. He had been to the other village to collect the lentil seeds.

The day my brother left, my father sat in the courtyard for a long time, looking at the night sky. Whenever he went through mental turmoil, he sat on one of the chairs in the yard and silently tried to get a solution to the problem.

My father had a false ego of fatherhood. He thought only about himself and his family. Also, he believed that other family members should follow whatever he said. He wanted to design everyone's life according to his imagination, like how a potter gives shape to his pots. But we have slowly drifted away from him, going away from his imaginative potter's wheel. The first one who left was my elder brother.

That is the reason I was not comfortable writing about my inconvenience or job to my elder brother. My mother forced me to write a letter to my brother every month. After writing about her well-being, she told me to write about myself, but I never wrote anything to my brother. I never wanted to discuss my job or the problems I was going through with my brother. I had a feeling that my brother never read the letters as he never gave a reply to us. Sometimes he wrote a letter or two in an entire year. But it's my father's order to write a letter to my brother each month. The letters should include details about the family, the sisters, the village and its weather conditions, and agriculture. According to my father, he is the family's eldest son, so he should know in detail about everything.

During hostel days, my father wrote at least one letter every month. He mentioned irrelevant details in the letter according to his thought and philosophy: A house doesn't mean a building made up of bricks and mortar, nor about the money saved. A home is built on faith, belief, and trust. A home is a belief. It has given shelter to human beings, their emotions, thoughts, and relationship. It is a place where each person depends on the other and shares a mutual bond.

I remembered my father's ethics until I got a temporary job in a private firm. Sometimes I also thought: I can never be able to leave my family, the crowd around it, my parents and uncle, and forget it. Among the controversies, there was mutual understanding and love. In a true sense, I had realized that within this chaos lived mutual love, the pleasure of being silent- I had already experienced this.

I never like the private firm where I was working. I missed my home. I felt like running into the home every day. Very often, I visited my home. It's almost four times a month, and as soon as I reach home, my mother worriedly looks at me and asks: How do you take your food? What have you made to your health?

Hearing what she says, many a time, I laugh at what she asks. To tease her, I ask: Do you think I am a small child? I am grown up now and settled like my brother. Tell me whether my brother is staying comfortably without you or not. Tell me.

My mother became silent. I never thought that my words would hurt her so much. She looked unhappy. She said: Let the goddess *Nistarini* bestow her blessings and keep him safe. This is what means the sacrifice of my mother. She will never think wrong about her children even though they don't enquire about her well-being and take care of her. Can a mother ever think sick about her children? During childhood, she tied the amulet in our hands to protect us from evil eyes. She always wished that we should be agile like a horse, more substantial like a tiger, defeat our enemies, and be ahead of everyone. Mothers all around the world must be like my mother. Who knows?

As the first fruit on the mango tree ripens, my mother will say: This is for my son. He will eat it. My son will have the biggest fish, fished from the pond. She never thought that her sons would ever go wrong. They are good, and others are responsible for spoiling them. This is my mother's philosophy!

It's difficult to get leave in private jobs. We had to work according to the owner's wish, but I went to my village whenever I could. In my workplace, I was always engrossed in my thoughts about my village.

I got rid of these thoughts because of *Rupashree*. She was working with me. We met in the office every day, but it took us almost one and a half years to come closer. *Rupashree*'s eyes were impossibly gorgeous. When we came closer, we discussed our house and family. I was overwhelmed and narrated to her about every member of my family.

Rupashree wept and said: You are lucky. You have your near and dear ones with you. But .....

I asked: Don't you have your family members?

Rupashree became emotional and in the same teary tone said: They are there but not so closely bonded. My father is an asthmatic patient, and my mother doesn't stay with us. She lives along with her parents in Kolkata. She is never worried; we have never visited our grandfather's house. My father has taken a lot of pain to raise children and educate us. I am the eldest and have two younger brothers and a sister. I am taking care of them because it's difficult for us to manage my father's pension and the land we have in the village. I must devote my entire life to them. Look at me... I have forgotten to dream, dream for myself at this age. Instead of looking beautiful, I look old.

I couldn't tolerate it as *Rupashree*'s beautiful eyes were filled with tears. I wiped her tears, embraced her, and said: Please don't cry. Everything will be fine.

After that, there was no formality between us, and we came closer. I left the mess where I stayed and lived in *Rupashree*'s house as a paying guest. There were no more problems regarding my food. *Rupashree* took care of me. She ironed my clothes and polished my shoes.

Once *Rupashree* said: Are you a paying guest in the house, or are you like a son-in-law?

I felt a little shy listening to this. *Rupashree* kissed me and said: Do you know, between us, I should have been a boy, and you should have been a girl.

I told my mother: I am taking my food to someone's house. My mother felt slightly relaxed but said: How long will you have food in others' houses? How long will the outsiders take care of you? We are old now. When will we have the privilege of having a daughter-in-law?

I wanted to say: Mother, I am currently taken care of by your would-be daughter-in-law, but I couldn't utter that.

My elder uncle's health had deteriorated by this time, and he was utterly dependent on others. He was sitting on his cot and was coughing the whole day in the front courtyard. He had a blurred vision. Many times, he scolded others for no reason. Sometimes my father sat with him and discussed something. My mother feared my uncle and didn't want to go near him to serve him food, but as my father scolded her, she nursed him including cleaning him from ablutions. My uncle wasn't at all satisfied with anything.

I was surprised to see the change in my uncle's behavior. Father said: My brother has grown old, and when a person becomes old, he behaves like a small kid. On that day, I went near him. He was sleeping. There was a musty and unpleasant smell emanating from his bed and room. I sat near his bed and called him softly: Uncle... uncle ....

Opening his eyes, he looked at me and behaved as if he didn't recognize me. I said: Uncle, I am ....

Uncle asked: Who are you? Then he glared at me. I think he recognized me. He got up from his bed and caressed me. He pulled out a book under his pillow, gave it to me, and said: Read it for me. I will listen. You are not visiting the village nowadays. Read... read....

I read:

Built the body with air and water.

Your body is like a deep forest...

It belongs to mother nature

Empowered through love ...

How much prudence it has ....

Dear God, you have given me this human body....

kept me under the sun

When I arrived, you put your hand on my forehead

And wrote my destiny.

The body is waiting to strike back,

When I leave this mortal world

Till I had the darshan of the God

How the body will remain...

My uncle again fell asleep. I thought my uncle had already slept, so I closed the book. My parents were standing near the door.

My uncle opened his eyes again, looked at me, and asked: Who are you?

Father said: He is your youngest son. Are you not able to recognize him?

He choked again and said: Where is the eldest son?

Father couldn't say anything. Uncle took a deep breath and couldn't say anything more. His eyes were open wide, and he flung his hand upward to catch something and withered in pain

My mother came near him and pressed his legs. Father said: Go quickly and call the *ayurvedic* doctor *Narayan Kabiraj*.

By the time *Narayan Kabiraj* came, my uncle was no more. My mother was crying, and my father was sitting silently. He was holding the *Bhagavat* in his hand. *Narayan Kabiraj* came and checked the pulse and heartbeat of my uncle. I asked *Narayan Kabiraj*: Is he alive? Please check him properly.

Narayan Kabiraj smiled and said: The swan has left the tree.

My father got up from his place and extinguished the lamp. He caught hold of me and wept like a small child… my world is over, I have become an orphan…

I could never believe that my father could cry like a small child. My mother was also surprised to see my father crying.

After some time, my father could control his emotions. He went out to call uncles and other relatives. Arrangements were made for the funeral. My mother took out the ten-year-old cow ghee and sandalwood from her box.

The *sankirtan* team (a team of devotional singers) sang the prayers ahead of others, and the most well-known devotional singer, my uncle's body was carried to the funeral, and my father silently walked next to his dead body like an innocent orphan child.

According to the ritual, my father shaved his head and was sad. When my aunt expired, my father was unhappy, but he wasn't shattered. He looked pretty old within ten days of my uncle's death. He lost weight as he ate once a day as per the rituals.

The cot in which my uncle used to sleep was s washed and kept in the courtyard. My father sat alone on that cot for a long time in the night and he was filled with sadness.

My mother was also silent. She was sitting silently for longer hours. The crowd in the house increased as my sisters, aunts, uncles, and sons-in-law came. The house became noisy. After the rituals on the tenth day, on the river bank, the relatives wore new clothes and returned home. They had their food at home. At night, my brother-in-law, who was from Cuttack, played the video. Excluding me and my parents, the rest others were having a fun time.

My brother and sister-in-law could not come from Delhi. My brother had sent a telegram. It was written: My son is suffering from pneumonia. I read the telegram and handed it over to my father. He tore the paper into pieces and said: The scoundrel is telling lies to his father. He is also a father and one day, he will realize the pain of a father. I was neither angry nor hated my brother. I forgave him, thinking that he was a materialistic character.

My father never asked me again about my elder brother. Sometimes my mother remembered him and waited for him eagerly waiting at the front door. As if someone is going to call her 'mother' from the front door! She only wiped her tears.

My father was trying to get accustomed to the noisy atmosphere at home to forget his sadness about the loss of his uncle. He played with his grandchildren of my cousins and took care of all the arrangements to be made for the food. He was enquiring about everyone's well-being.

But I didn't like the noisy atmosphere. I wanted to sit quietly and remember my uncle, but relatives were in the house, and the atmosphere was noisy.

On a moonlit night, my father and I sat on the cot on which my uncle used to sleep. My mother was cooking for everyone and gossiping with sister Hema, Moti Aunty, and Kuni and the children were already asleep.

There was silence in the house. I looked at the night sky. After sitting quietly, my father said: When are you leaving?

I said: Tomorrow.

It was for the first time my father said: Why don't you stay back for a few more days? Will there be any problem?

I said: As you wish.

My father said with remorse: This house will be deserted if you leave. In this house of straw, your mother and I, like two birds, will feel lonely- will sit around looking at each other's faces. All of you will learn and fly away from here like birds searching for your destination. Searching for a new tree, you will build your own nest, and ultimately, your children will learn how to fly. One fine day, they will leave your nest, searching for their destination and companion.

My father couldn't utter anything more. I couldn't believe my ears as I listened to my father. Did my father say this? Or the darkness or the cot on which my uncle slept?

The mix of *Mogra* flower fragrance with the moonlight made the night more mysterious.

I was thinking about my father and the house he has set up with so much enthusiasm. It is the house treasured with memories of my childhood, teenage and youth. The place where my mother's household chore is never over, where my father tries to show his authority, and my uncle enlightens everyone with his knowledge.

Now three of us were there in that house. My mother was in the kitchen, and I sat with my father on the cot.

Oh! Uncle! Where are you? Are you there in heaven or the abode of Vishnu *(Baikuntha)?* You are miles away from us. Wherever you are, stay in bliss.

I will return to my workplace, the city, or you can say to *Rupashree*'s house the day after tomorrow or the next day. Will my parents agree if I get married to *Rupashree*? If they disagree, will I marry her and forget my parents and family? *Rupashree* can never stay in our house after marriage because she has an ailing father and siblings whom she takes care of. What will happen to the dream of my mother, who dreamt about a daughter-in-law?

Can I be selfish like my elder brother?

Neither I nor my parents could sleep properly that night. My mother was sitting near the doorway and was engrossed in her thoughts, whereas my father was lying on the cot and gazing at the night sky.

I wasn't able to sleep and was feeling restless. It was

almost dawn by the time I could muster some sleep. My father woke me up and said: Why will you stay back in this house? It's better if you go back to your workplace. You can visit us later on.

I was also waiting to get out of that gloomy atmosphere. I took a bath and was ready to leave. Mother sobbed and asked: When will you come again?

I said: Next week.

Father said: You have already taken leave for a fortnight. Can you get leave again?

I thought that was true. I told a lie to make my mother happy. I didn't speak anything much.

My father came along with me to the bus stand. We didn't discuss anything much. The bus arrived, and I boarded the bus.

My father was standing there. Though he was silent, still, I could understand from his expression that he was asking me: When will you come again?

I was sentimental and felt I should get off the bus, hold my father's feet and ask him: Why did you teach me to fly? Why didn't you cut my wings? With what hope and what kind of sky-touching dreams did you make me educated? Why didn't you teach me to plow the field, sow seeds, take care of the openings in the paddy fields with an umbrella on top on rainy days; plant banana saplings on the edges of ponds; to leave fish seedlings in the pond? For what reasons did you educate these false things and made me fly??

Please don't look at me in that way, dear father. I am helpless….

The bus left the bus stop.

My father was still staring at me. After some time, I couldn't see my father. Our eyes were filled with tears.

While doing *sankirtan* (oratorical singing) on the village streets; arranging offerings *(Jagyna)* to the sky for the clouds; offering *chitou pitha* (Indian Rice Pan Cake) in the paddy fields; while repairing the river embankment to protect the village from the floods; while arbitrating and deciding on the village fights; while answering the queries related to sinful pregnancy of unwed village girls by the village quacks *(Kalesi)*; while driving out the dreaded angry ox from the ripe paddy fields; while listening to the tune of the song " Today, I saw a young damsel" from the flute of cattle rearer *Krushna Behera* through the meadows filled with the fragrance of screw pine and pandanus odorifier *(Ketaki)* flowers around the *Jogi* hills amongst jackfruit trees, butternut trees, blueberry trees and mango trees; while offering the alms to the village deity Mother *Mangalaa* to protect people from the anguish of goddesses responsible for chicken px, measles, dysentery and other contagious diseases, the children of the village grew up to become young man; the young man turning to be adults; adults turning into old people and old people having their journey to the graveyards.

While playing swing on the tree branches, hide and seek, game of dice, playful cards, ludo, and even cricket, I always remembered my village.

But what was there for me in that village? There was a river, a few old banyan trees, the altar of the goddesses, the bank of the river, the altar of goddess *Mangala* near the riverside, and a pond filled with aquatic plants. These attractions were slowly fading away from my consciousness. I was growing to be an adult in between remembering and forgetting things.

Whenever I returned to the village, I remembered my minor days. I only sighed! *Aha!* Where are those golden days of childhood?

I had four sisters and a brother. Still, my grandmother was sad that we were very few children in the house. She always told my mother that Lord *Krishna* was the eighth child of *Devaki*, but my mother was not fit to conceive anymore for the eighth time. My father loved and scolded us a lot, but he also used to take us to fairs and festivals. He taught us different forms of Sanskrit grammar during the night, and my mother served us food together. We would fight during dinner. My elder brother was like the ringleader. He bossed over the siblings by using brute force. We all slept together at night except *Kuni*, as she was the youngest one. She slept with my mother and was the apple of my mother's eye.

My mother used to sing for us. She also told us the stories of small children who went to the forest and worshipped god relentlessly so that they could meet god. Once I told my mother that I would also worship god with devotion to meet him. My mother's eyes were filled with tears when she heard this. She said: Don't say it like this. May god bless you for many long years.

My grandmother was always dissatisfied with everything. She would be doing something or the other all the time. She would clean the rice by removing the stones, kill the caterpillars of the drumstick tree, or else would be cursing my mother. Very often, she picked up a quarrel with the neighbors for trivial reasons. She would take up a fight with neighbors for their chicks spoiling our spinach fields. Sometimes she would weep remembering her late husband (our grandfather). She would be elated seeing us around her and would give me a coin of fifty *paise* to run to the shop and get tobacco for her, and I would purchase the tobacco for half of the amount given by her and, with the rest, buy lemon candies. We would all sit together, relish the sweets, and would be conspiring to plan how to cheat and deceive her to get more money from her purse.

My father was a hard nut to crack. He wanted everything to be done timely like eating on time, reading during reading hours, playing during breaks, and sleeping when it's time to go to bed. Can the children adhere to this strict timing? But my father could never understand that. Sometimes we felt that father had never gone through his childhood. Whenever my father would get angry, my mother supported us. Of course, my grandmother was always there in favor of us, but sometimes, when my mother supported us, she would switch her side. I never liked this dual attitude of my grandmother. Whenever I complained about this to my elder brother, he would make me understand that my father and uncle were the sons of our grandmother. All of us get surprised by this matter.

If we switched on the radio, my grandmother would ask us to switch it off. She would say it's too noisy. We are bound to stop the radio. It was a strict instruction from my father that we all should listen to what our grandmother says. She is the head of the house and the eldest of all. Sometimes we thought that our father, who is short-tempered and cruel (of course for us), why was so scared of grandmother. That is a mystery within us.

My elder brother studied in a school four miles away from our village. My mother often requested my father: Please purchase a bicycle for him. The kid is walking such a longer distance. My father didn't heed it and said: Ten more children attend school. Is he the only one? If he walks and goes, then his legs will become stronger. My grandmother once said: Listen, a machine has come in which some small are showing tricks. Why don't you bring one? I am an old lady and want to see that.

My father brought home television that week. My grandmother was happy. She sat and watched the television. Neither did she get irritated with anyone nor quarreled with anyone after that. Sometimes she would call us: Come quickly and see an excellent game. Come quickly. She addressed all the programs on television as games. In the beginning, my mother wasn't happy with it; later, maybe she forgot and sat with my grandmother to enjoy watching television.

My mother always behaved like a typical village woman. Her paternal house was in the Gadajat area (*an area ruled by the king and normally had a Gad (fort)*). My maternal grandfather and my uncle *Sapuni* used to visit our house. My grandfather was a jovial person. His bag carried a sandalwood stick, a hand mirror, beads, and a framed photo of god smeared with sandal paste. My mother was always in high spirits whenever my grandfather visited. Father would take his bicycle and go to the market to get eggs, as Grandfather was fond of country egg curry.

At night while going to sleep, my grandfather narrated the *Gadjat* stories. He told us the story of a *Paika* (warrior) who could overpower ten *Britishers* only with a stick, how the ghosts of the hilly region are taller than the trees, and how a ghost named '*Haadabaai*' would destroy rice pots by putting human excreta.

My grandfather would still be coughing despite all of us falling asleep listening to his stories, but my mother would still be awake. She would discuss her family matters with my grandfather. How my elder maternal uncle went to Assam and settled down there after marriage. *Sapuni* uncle is the only hope for my grandfather. Still, it was only *Sapuni* uncle who stayed back with my grandfather. *Sapuni* uncle was inclined towards theatre; according to him, he can earn his living by acting in operas.

My grandfather would say: No one could make it. If I would wake up in between and go straight to my grandfather, he would make me sit on his lap and tell my mother 'Listen! This grandson of mine will be a well-educated officer. His eyes are reflecting the same.

I was unable to understand what he meant by Deputy (Officer)!

We all had a lovely time whenever *Sapuni* uncle came. My mother would get irritated with his demeanor. He would deliver the dialogues of the play in front of us. My father would say: *Sapuni*, I have arranged your job. *Sapuni* uncle would laugh and say sarcastically: Do you think I will do a job? How can you tell an artist to do a job? That's not possible.

We would appreciate *Sapuni* uncle and mumble: What a powerful dialogue delivery!

Sapuni uncle would ignore whatever my mother said with a whisker. Our mother was also a strange person! It was tough to understand my mother. She scolded *Sapuni* uncle as he was interested in theatre. On the contrary, she would bring small fish from the fisherman's village and prepare fish with mustard paste loved the preparation.

Sapuni uncle would tell me: Listen young man! I don't get along well with your mother. If she can convince our father, he will sell the land and give me thirty thousand rupees, and I can establish a theatre company. I am sure it will create a sensation in Bengal, Odisha, and Bihar. Leave it; it's not in my fate.

Words like Bengal, Bihar, and Odisha sounded uncanny to me, that is the reason I liked *Sapuni* uncle so much.

In the evening, *Sapuni* uncle and I smoked Bidi without anyone's knowledge. If I coughed a bit, *Sapuni* uncle would scold me and say: Worthless boy, can't you smoke properly?

Those who don't smoke Bidi.

His clan is a horse-faced one.

CHAPTER 2

My elder brother went to Cuttack for further studies, and I joined the high school. Coughing a lot, my maternal grandfather died one day. I joined the last rites of my grandfather; removed all my hair and did the offering to the Sun god. My grandmother, who looks like a goddess by adorning herself with a lot of jewelry and beautiful sarees, was now in a white saree. She hugged me and cried incessantly. I cried, but my elder brother didn't. I scolded him and said: Heartless fellow.

In the meantime, *Sapuni* uncle was taking care of the fields and cultivation. Hairless, he was sitting quietly and smoking bidi.

My maternal grandmother passed away a few days after my grandfather's death. After that, our relationship with my maternal uncle's house loosened a bit. By the time I completed my studies in high school and joined college, my brother was already engaged in a job in Delhi.

All my younger sisters got married. My uncle's daughter *Saakhi* sister was burnt alive by her in-laws, and receiving the telegram, my elder brother came from Delhi. He insisted on lodging a complaint and filing a case, but my elder uncle refused. He said: She left this mortal world as it was already time for her to go. My brother was annoyed, he scolded them in English, and the next day, he left for Delhi.

I stayed in the college hostel, but I was disturbed as

I didn't like the atmosphere. I wrote a letter to my father: I remember you all and the village. I am thinking of not continuing my studies further and going back to the village.

My father, instead of giving a reply to my letter, came to the hostel. My mother had sent puffed rice and some sweet pancakes. I had the sweet pancakes along with my friends. I remembered my mother and cried. My father brought me closer to him and said: If you study well and become a good human being, then I and the people in the village will feel proud of you. This is also a desire of your mother. Instantly I was angry with my mother. After giving birth to so many children, shouldn't she think about keeping them closer to her? My elder and younger sisters cried when they got married, and so also my mother echoed with their weeping, but after they went to their in-laws' house, they forgot my mother. Mother also forgot them!

Now I could realize that my mother was trying to forget me again, I thought so but could not speak this to my father.

Dragging his slippers, Father left the hostel to return to the village, and I went to drop him at the bus stop. He boarded the bus, but I could see tears dangling in his eyes. Why was he crying? I couldn't understand how a stone-hearted person like my father could cry. Was he crying? Why? For what?

By the time I completed my education at the university, my father wasn't that old. Still, my mother looked a little older because of the hard work that she did to manage the house. After completing my studies, I stayed in the house, attended the interviews, and appeared for the competitive examinations.

During that time, my elder brother married one of his colleagues in Delhi. My father was furious when he received the invitation card. He scolded my mother and said: What will the people in the village, the relatives say when they will come to know about the marriage? My daughters, sons-in-law, and I don't know anything about the wedding. What type of marriage is this? What does he think about me? I disown my son.

My mother said: Forgive him. He is immature. Why are you making it a big issue? My grandmother had grown too old by that time. She had no work other than interfering in all the matters and finding mistakes. She said: It's okay if he gets married, but what is the girl's caste? Is she a Christian girl? If so, then our ancestors will not be able to get their due respect.

My elder aunt said: There is a saying, different religions, and different customs. It doesn't matter to which faith she belongs, but once she is married into our family, she belongs to our caste and clan.

My grandmother asked: How?

My father calmed down by the evening. In the evening, my mother told me to write a letter to my brother. She said: Write that we are all happy after listening to his marriage and ask him to come to the village with our daughter-in-law.

My mother was so strange a person! She would know everything; would understand right and wrong and yet would not wish to make anyone feel hurt. I was very much annoyed with my brother as he devoid me of the love of my sister-in-law.

After receiving the letter, my brother came home

along with my sister-in-law. She wasn't able to speak Odia properly. My mother liked my sister-in-law and bestowed her love and affection on her. She gifted her necklace though it was of an old design. My mother could understand from her expression that she didn't like it and said: This is made of solid gold. You can exchange it and purchase another necklace of your choice. My sister-in-law was happy. She roamed happily inside the house.

My sister-in-law gifted a shawl to my grandmother, and she was pleased. She supported her and said: You are such a pretty girl.

My father came to know that my sister-in-law belonged to a Brahmin family. He didn't tell anything to my brother and went to the pond in the backyard with a net, for fishing. My brother wanted to speak to my father but was hesitating as he was angry. My father called me, and I went along with him for fishing. He said: It was only for his marriage I didn't allow anyone to catch fish from the pond. I was listening to him without saying anything.

We could get four big fish. After lunch, my brother called me and asked: What are you planning to do?

I replied: I am appearing for competitive examinations and attending the interviews, but I am yet to crack anything.

He said: You should get engaged in a job as soon as possible. Father is growing old. You have to take responsibility for the house. He spoke as if he had no duties and inclination toward the family. I didn't like it but remained silent.

The next day my brother and sister-in-law left. My sister-in-law gave me two notes of hundred rupees at the station and said: Whenever you find time, visit us.

I told my father that my sister-in-law gave me two hundred rupees. He was annoyed and said: Why didn't you throw that money on her face? He mumbled something and left saying- she is showing me money!

My mother didn't say anything.

That evening my father sat in the courtyard for a long time on a chair. My mother went near him and said: Won't you sleep tonight?

Father didn't say anything.

She shook my father and asked: Are you listening to me? Suddenly she screamed: You have a high temperature. Why are you sitting outside in this cold?

My father said: The boy came home after so many days. I didn't speak to him, and he left. I am still determining when he will come again.

I wanted to call the village doctor at night, but my father didn't allow me. He sat in front of me like an unsolved puzzle.

I had to leave the village as I got an offer of a private job. My father didn't say anything. My mother sobbed and said: Couldn't you become an officer or a judge after studying so much? Where will you go and stay, and how will you have food?

I laughed and said: Why are you sobbing? Am I a small child?

She didn't say anything. I didn't look back as I knew my mother would cry. She went to the village temple, offered the *puja*, and brought the sacred cloth and vermilion of the goddesses and kept it in my suitcase. I took my bag and left the house. I knew she must be crying behind me. My father accompanied me to the bus stand. He gave me five hundred rupees and said: Take care of your health. Don't worry about money. Job is not more important than health. It's a new place with a different climate, so if the weather conditions don't suit you, you can come back home. The holy book says- this body is surely the foremost instrument of doing [good] deeds

The bus arrived and left.

I looked through the big window of the bus at my father. He wasn't crying. He was standing silently on the road like a father.

My father stood similarly on the road the day my brother left for Delhi. I was a boy at that time. My elder brother used to hit me a lot, but still, I felt like crying when he left, but my father didn't cry. On our way home, he said: One day, you will leave us and go to Bombay or Madras for a job. You will also earn a lot of money and become rich. You will travel in an airplane.

I said: No.

It was foggy, and I couldn't see my father. I looked at my village, roads, and paddy fields; remembered the poem of Sachi Routray, and also thought about my mother.

My mother must be sitting alone silently. Father will return home tired and sit on the veranda. My mother won't ask anything but will sob. On his own, my father would tell her: The bus arrived an hour late. He boarded the bus. I told him to return home if he didn't feel good there. It's not okay to do a job at the cost of health. My mother wouldn't give a reply and enter the prayer room to pray for my well-being for a very long time.

I know that she won't feel like cooking. She will cook some rice and burn the lentils. My father always complains even if the food is prepared well. He says: This isn't good, that is not good, but today he will have his food silently without complaining. My mother would ask him: in a whispering tone, Didn't you like the food? He would say: Everything is tasty today, but I have a little bit of stomach upset.

In the afternoon, he will read lying on his bed and won't sleep. A yogi would be singing:

Pray the name of the lord Remember, son;

Pray the name of lord Ram;

If you can't do this,

The apple of the clan

The God of Death (Yama) will tie and take you away

My mother would be wiping her tears with her veil, and my father's eyes would be filled with tears. The yogi would sing *Tika Govinda Chandra* for an hour. His song will get over but not the tears from my mother's eyes.

The bus would jump tree after tree; village after village; town after town, crossings after crossings. The bus will alight old people and forget them; will start calling new people … come …come

By the time I reached my destination, it would be seven in the evening yet I will not feel about the long period. I will get off the bus and take a rickshaw.

Rupashee was in love with me from her side. She wrote the first letter to me from her side. Rupashee was beautiful and worked as a steno in the firm where I got an appointment. She asked me first: Will you continue your job in this private firm, or are you preparing for any other career? She was the one who offered me food in the office and said: Don't think that you are away from the family, so you are alone on this earth.

Truly, I remembered my mother at that moment when she told this me, but I tried to hide my tears and smiled. *Rupashree* said: Your smile is infectious.

I visited my home during every holiday. My brother had stopped visiting us. One of his sons had caught Pneumonia in the village, so my sister-in-law didn't want to return to the village again.

My mother had sent some *Ayurvedic* medicine and bison urine to Delhi. Also, she wrote in the letter to give the medication to the child on an empty stomach as he was suffering from pneumonia. Still, my mother couldn't know whether the child was cured. My brother bought a plot in North Delhi and was building a house.

My father was reciting Bhagwat Geeta that night, and my holidays were over, but as my mother cried, I had to stay back for two more days. My father was reading the tenth chapter. It was written that Vasudev, on that stormy and rainy night, picked up the infant and carried him in a big basket on his head. The snake *Basuki* had covered the basket with his fang. My father had a sweet voice, and my uncle wanted that he should be an oratorio singer like him. Still, my father wasn't interested in that. He was motivated by the ideology of Gandhiji. He went from village to village singing national poet *Birakishore's* songs and collected a handful of rice from each house. My uncle was annoyed and said: You are going against the Britishers; they are like our God. It's better if you stay separately.

My father laughed and said: All these properties belong to you. You can take everything but don't say those white-skinned people are God. If they are our God, then what is the dignity of our lord *Purushottam*?

My uncle became quiet. After some time, he said: Do whatever you want.

Father was reading Bhagwat Geeta with full devotion. My mother was leaning on the wall, sobbing and wiping her tears. I was lying on the bed listening to my father's reading. Suddenly I fell asleep. When I woke up, I could hear him reading the eighth chapter, where King *Kansa* was trying to kill the eighth child, a girl given birth by *Devaki*.

My mother said: You may stop reading now. I have already finished cooking, so you can have your food now.

After some time, I, along with my father, had food. My father broke his silence and said: Do you think your job will be permanent in the future?

I nodded and said: Yes, but it may take some time.

Father said: Don't worry. Your brother has written in the letter that he got a promotion. Your sister-in-law is expecting a baby. Why don't you go to Delhi at least once? He may be feeling lonely in such a big city.

I was annoyed with my brother because he never wrote me a letter, and thinks he is the most learned person on earth. He is very good at giving advice, so sometimes he speaks like an old man. Will he be happy to see me? He may start explaining to me about the shares in the stock market, how the price is increasing, and which insurance policy gives the maximum benefit. It will be too dull. Does he remember our childhood, how we played and visited the fair? Does he remember *Sapani* uncle, grandfather, mother, and father? They may not be vital to him.

Then why will I visit the brother?

My father's eyes were filled with tears. He would say: Is it possible for me to see all of you at this old age? Instead, all of you should visit us on your own and try to learn about our well-being.

He would say this and get up from his place with an incomplete meal. As it was summer, the mogra plant was blooming with flowers, and the courtyard would be filled with the sweet smell of mogra.

I sat on the cot and looked at the sky. The sky seemed to be the same as it was in my childhood. The same number of stars in the sky. The stars were twinkling in the sky like before. There was no change at all. Almost same.

I wanted to smoke, but as my father was there, so I hesitated. I lay down and looked at the sky.

I was feeling sleepy. My mother came and sat next to me and said: Get married soon. I want to enjoy the food prepared by my daughter-in-law in this old age. Do you think I would work so hard like this until my death? I smiled. She again said: Can't you hear what I am saying?

I said: Do you think that I am deaf?

My mother said: If you want to marry, let us know. We will look for a bride. I said: Why? Can't I find a girl for myself? She remained quiet. I felt a little guilty. I thought that I shouldn't have spoken to her rudely.

My mother wanted her daughter-in-law to stay with her, learn the rituals, and should take care of the house. She also desired her daughter-in-law to read Bhagwat Geeta for her, wear anklets and move around in the house, and the courtyard to be filled with the tinkling sound of the anklet. I also wanted the same. I wasn't a stone-hearted person like my brother.

While leaving the village for the town, to my working place, like every time, Father also came to drop me at the bus stand. This time, Father didn't talk much with me, I felt as if the father has grown old a bit more in between.

The bus was late, and we sat under a tree. Then he said: Your mother cannot do so much work anymore, and she is always cribbing for a daughter-in-law. But don't take her words so seriously and do whatever you feel is good for you. She doesn't have any idea about the difficulties in a job.

I looked at my father's face. Sadness reflected in his eyes, and he looked at the end of the black tar road. The road which leads to my destination, the city where I live, and I will be able to revisit him only after maybe after four or six months or a year or so.

Remorsefully, Father said: Your brother has already

purchased land and constructed his house in Delhi, so he will probably settle there. What will happen to the land, the house in the village? Hiding me, He tried to wipe off his tears. After some time, he laughed and said: I could not see my grandson in Delhi. If he had brought him once, we could have seen him. As per him, the village atmosphere is unsuitable for his children. Didn't you all grow up in this atmosphere? None of you suffered from Pneumonia. This science has made you all fragile inside. Your generation doesn't believe and is not devoted to God. Not weather alone, even ants will make you scared now.

The bus arrived, and I boarded the bus hurriedly. My father was still standing there. Breathlessly, the bus started running leaving the village, roads, paddy fields, and my father behind. I wasn't interested in looking outside the bus. I closed my eyes and tried to take a nap.

I thought: I will go and give my resignation in the office and return to my village. I will look after the fields in the village along with my father, will go with my father to the pond to clean it, will sleep near my mother and trouble her like a child, and will listen to her stories from her. She will chew beetle like my grandmother and start narrating the stories: Once there was a quarrel between Lord *Shiva* and *Parvati*. At that time, *Parvati* had only one son *Kartikeya*. She was annoyed and went to *Kartikeya* and said: Son, I fought with your father, so I won't stay with him. I will stay with you, but *Kartikeya* said 'No'. *Parvati* started crying because of this, and then *Naarad* arrived. He said you could have stayed with him if you had another son. If one son supports the father, the other will support the mother. Listening to this, Goddesses *Parvati* carved an idol of a boy out of turmeric powder and breathed life into it, unbeknownst to her husband, Lord *Shiva*. He stayed along with Goddesses *Parvati*. She asked *Ganesh* to guard the door of the house for her. She told him not to let anyone pass him, no matter who they were… *Ganesh* sacrificed his head for the head of an elephant.

Finally, the bus stopped and I reached my destination,

Rupashree said: I am unable to manage the house anymore. The responsibility of the house suffocates me. Kindly help me out, please. Make me free from all this.

I said: Listen! Rupa, what can be done immediately? I have to write a letter to my parents and get their permission. I am also still preparing for it.

Rupashree's eyes were filled with tears.

I wrote a letter to my father that I would visit them when I got the leave.

Rupashree insisted that she would also go along with me to the village. I couldn't deny her. *Rupashree* went along with me to the village. My father was waiting at the bus stand. *Rupashree* touched my father's feet and took his blessings. I didn't mention anything in the letter regarding *Rupashree*, so my father looked at me in surprise. I also felt a little uneasy. *Rupashree* introduced herself and said: My name is *Rupashree*. We are working together in the same office. We have a long holiday of five days, that's why I came to meet you and to enjoy the beauty of the village. My father smiled. Three of us walked silently, and to break the silence, my father said: This time, there wasn't a good production of lentils. The insects destroyed a large part of it. The weather is also not conducive, and there is no rain.

That was the time when the dark clouds came from

the east. *Rupashree* looked at it and said: It's going to rain heavily.

Father said the sky is cloudy, but it won't rain. The clouds will be drifted away by the western wind. There is a proverb: Thunderous clouds don't shower.

By the time we reached home, it was almost evening. My mother was lighting the lamp. My father entered the house and shouted: Where are you? Look! Who has come?

Mother came outside. My father, slightly startled after meeting *Rupashree*, said they both work in the same office. Then he told *Rupashree* to go inside the house.

My mother didn't say anything and looked at me.

It rained heavily that night. I looked outside the window of my old study room. There was lightning, and I could see the trees outside between the flashes of lightning.

I remembered my childhood. On such a rainy day, my brother and I would sit in the room, and my father would sit and weave the mat on the veranda, or he would discuss the sacred scriptures with others. We could hear the loud voice of my father while discussing the scriptures.

Devoid of eating any food!

Free from sexual orientation

Whenever hungry or thirsty

Doesn't drink milk and water

Dust doesn't touch the body.

Looks grandeur in appearance

Appears whenever sleeps or dozes off,

Sleeps on the platform;

He who doesn't have a figurine,

Who is not humane

Who doesn't have hands and legs like us

Who doesn't sleep is not the body

Oh lord of the common man

He is the soul and he is the supreme!!

My mother would try to control her laugh and say: Your father should leave the family, become a saint and stay in the ashram.

We could never understand the content of what my father spoke. My brother said: His friend's father's heart was transplanted. All these unnecessary talks about the soul and its existence are false. My Brother was in college. He usually speaks these crap things to show his superiority to others, but I like what my father says. My father is right in understanding life and soul, whereas my brother doesn't know anything. He is just trying to boast.

My father's deliberations and tenor continue till the wee hours of the night. When my father started preaching, the time passes quickly. In between, there would be a discussion about the village, the weather, the crops, and the insects spoiling the lentil fields; stories about the *sankirtan* singer *Budhiaa* grandfather of a nearby village, and also about *Udhab Sahu*.

Father's stories never end. My mother would wait for him to have his food and try to draw his attention by knocking on the door several times, jingling with her bangles, by incessant coughing but she could never draw my father's attention. She would become angry and send my elder brother to call him for dinner.

My father would say: Oh! *Loknath* and *Jadua bhai*, you can go now. It's already late; we will again continue with the discussion tomorrow about the clan of *Jadu*.

When my father would sit for dinner, my mother would show her annoyance and says: Are you not aware of the time? It's already late, and the food is cold. What do you get from these long discussions?

My father would laugh and say: A person born as a woman doesn't know about religiousness and non-religiousness.

Mother would make a funny face.

My brother and I would sit quietly, listening to them and enjoying them. It would be raining heavily, and we would sleep after dinner. Father would sleep along with us.

We will not be into a deep sleep; he would say: Children! Are you scared of thunderstorms and lightning outside? This rain and thunderstorm are not so ferocious. In *Gopa*, the shower and thunderstorm were very furious, as it was planned by Lord Indra. Lord Krishna, who was almost your age, lifted the mountain with his tiny finger and saved the people of *Gopa.*

Our eyes will be filled with sleep, The photograph of Lord Krishna hanging in the puja room would come into my mind.

It was raining, and the village was flooded with water. There will be a water stream in the village street-completely red with the colors from the roof. Despite this, I didn't go outside and sat inside the house quietly.

Mother was working in the kitchen, and *Rupashree* sat beside her. *Rupashree* had already impressed my mother.

It's effortless to impress my mother, which I mostly did in childhood. I thought Mother had also developed feelings for *Rupashree* in these few hours. She was discussing with her about the family and how they are closely knit. She told her about the love and affection that her elder son and daughter-in-law show towards her. How they write her letters every month and send her gifts. I knew that my mother was lying. She never spoke ill about her children in front of others- that is her consecration.

Rupashree came near me when I was sitting quietly in that darkness. She came and leaned on my shoulder. I could feel her breath and her tears, and my heart softened. For some unknown reason, I also felt like crying.

Rupashree said: I don't want to leave this place, especially your mother. You are lucky as you have your mother along with you.

I glared at *Rupashree* and could see the tears in her eyes in that dim light.

Suddenly she said: Please don't throw me out of this house anytime. Please, promise me.

In that dim light, she looked like a goddess. Bright and Beautiful. I could understand from her expression that she wasn't lying. I kissed her and said: Everything will be fine.

We all had dinner together, and I could see my mother's eyes brimming with tears. I could understand that she was remembering my brother. For a long time, he didn't come home, didn't sit with us to have food together, or complained about the food.

I could understand: Mother wanted all the family members in the house. She wanted to spend her time with her son, daughter-in-law, and grandchildren. She wanted a complete family, but we wanted to be away from the family and the root.

I wasn't feeling sleepy that night. I could listen to the pitter-patter of the raindrops and the croaking of the frogs. *Rupashree* was sleeping with my mother in the other room, and both were whispering. Maybe my mother was narrating some story she told me during my childhood. I knew *Rupashree* would get bored of these stories and fall asleep after a while.

There was no rain by the next day early morning, and the sky was clear. It was twilight, and the moon illuminated the sky below the horizon. The house had a lot of humidity, so I came out to the courtyard, filled with Mogra's sweet smell. I pulled a chair, sat, and smoked. I couldn't smoke before my father from the day I came home. There was a peculiar smell that was around due to the mixing of both Mogra and cigarette smell.

After some time, my mother woke up and come to the courtyard. She looked at me and asked, why are you sitting outside now? Won't you catch a cold?

I said: I am feeling good. Is *Rupashree* sleeping?

Mother smiled and said: Yes. She is a nice girl. I want a daughter-in-law like her. Mother smiled like the clean moonlighted night,

I had a passing thought- Should I tell my mother that *Rupashree* is your would-be daughter-in-law? She will be there with you lifelong. You can narrate her stories like *Kuni* sister; she will read *Bhagabat* and *Ramayan* to you. She will leave her job and look after you. She is like your loving daughter.

Mother said: I am making it very clear to you that on the following auspicious day for marriage, I will get you married, and if you disagree, then I will swallow poison. Will you get married and send us on a pilgrimage or not? Who wants to suffer in this old age?

I smiled and said: I will do whatever you say.

Her eyes were filled with tears, but this time, it was the tears of happiness.

By the time *Rupashree* woke up, she had come and sat with us. She plucked a fistful of Mogra flowers, held those in her hands, and sniffed.

Mother said: Why do you sniff the flowers in that way? There may be insects that may harm you.

Rupashree laughed, put the flowers in mother's lap, rested her head on my mother's lap, and said: I will sleep here. It's too humid inside.

The three days of holidays were over within no time. I felt like staying back in the house for a few more days. *Rupashree* suggested sending a leave application to extend the Casual leaves.

I said 'No' and whispered in her ears: Are you planning to stay back here permanently?

Rupashree blushed.

We returned to the city where we worked. My father came with us to the bus stand but was relatively silent. I could feel that my father was shattered from within. He was young, but instead of wearing the *Ambica* mill dhoti and the shawl this time, he was in *Khorda* towels.

He didn't give his valuable advice to me. Maybe by this time, he knew that I had become a major.

As soon as we boarded the bus, he left. Is he annoyed with me? I thought about it and was in remorse.

Rupashree was sitting next to me and was looking outside the window. We left behind our village. It became invisible slowly inside a fistful of smoke and a blue sky. I looked at *Rupashree*. She was crying.

I asked: Why are you crying?

She kept her head on my shoulder and said: I am remembering your mother.

Her unkempt hair flew in the air to brush against my face. My mother had applied a lot of oil on her hair and had said strictly to keep oiling the hair or else the hair will turn grey faster. She had also double-plaited *Rupashree's* ponytail hair. Now *Rupashree's* age had receded to that of a school-going girl.

I said to *Rupashree*: You look very sexy.

She pinched me naughtily and said: You are a liar.

Rupashrree said: My father is trying to get me married somewhere else. Please do something; otherwise, your *Rupashree* will be dead forever.

I could see tears in her eyes. I said: I must write a letter to my parents. I have to take their permission. My father will come and meet your father and give the proposal. He will also match our horoscopes and fix an auspicious day for our marriage.

Rupashree said: These are old tales, old sentiments. If you stick to those, you are going back to ancient times. If you don't do something sooner, then even though I don't want; still have to get married to the person my father has selected, or I have to commit suicide.

I became sentimental as I saw *Rupashree* crying. I knew we couldn't live without each other.

I had to arrange something. I must write a letter to my father and inform him: Father, I have arranged my marriage myself, and you no longer have to take that responsibility. I am marrying *Rupashree*, who went with me to the village during summer vacation. I seek your blessings. Never before I have done anything before without your consent. Still, we are getting married on a so-and-so date in *Arya Mandap*. Please attend our marriage.

I have to write to my mother: I have found a daughter-in-law for you. She is *Rupashree*. You applied coconut oil on her hair and plaited it. She is the same girl who never wanted to leave you and come to the city. That girl will become your daughter-in-law. Hope you will attend our marriage.

My father will receive the letter. Will he be sad and subdued? Will his eyes be filled with tears? He will read the letter in front of my mother who will sob quietly. Father will tear the letter into pieces; leave the house for village roads. Mother will look at the black and white graduation photograph on the wall and murmur: So, you are grown up enough to get married according to your own choice?

Will both of my parents come to my wedding or not? No, they will come.

My mother will come. If my father disagrees, she will become stubborn and try to convince him. I know that my father is a hard nut to crack. He will get angry at my mother's stubbornness and say: I don't have any son. If at any time I had sons, then at this moment, I disown them. He will say this and start coughing. My father gets a cough when he is in too much tension.

Mother will say: I will go. How can my youngest son be getting married, and I won't go? I will go. If you don't want, then you can't. I will go alone. Just help me to board the bus.

Father will sit quietly for a day. The next day he will sell lentils, paddy, and two acres of land; arrange the money and say: If you want to go, get ready. I don't want to see his face, but I must go to protect my dignity and reputation.

Mother will collect all her jewelry and say: Let's go.

But nothing like that happened. I just sent a telegram to my father that I am getting married, but my parents didn't come. After a long wait, *Rupashree*'s maternal uncle got us married. The marriage wasn't an elaborate celebration. I left my rented premise and shifted to *Rupashree*'s house.

Rupashree's father said: Son, Is your father so cruel? He didn't come to his son's marriage. Is he not happy with your marriage? Isn't it one kind of offense?

I told *Rupashree*: Let's go to the village. My parents must be worried. I know that when my brother got married at that time, my parents were concerned. My father suppresses his feelings, but my mother can't. She must be crying. Let's go.

Rupashree remained quiet after listening and then said: We took leave recently for our marriage, so we won't get any break now, and other than that if you want, you may go. Your parents didn't attend the wedding, and I have my self-respect. Will it be good if I go?

I wanted to tell *Rupashree* about my elder brother and sister-in-law. My father still doesn't speak to my brother, but when he visits, he goes to the pond to catch fish and arranges everything my brother likes to eat. I wanted to tell her how my mother would be weeping alone in that house.

She mightn't be going to the riverbank to take a bath to avoid the women in the village discussing her son and daughter-in-law. She must be performing various pujas and praying for our well-being. My parents must be worried thinking about us. Maybe we will arrive without notice. She must be inattentive while serving food to my father. She must have overcooked rice, put lots of water in the lentil soup, and missed putting salt into the curry. Hiding from my father, she must be wiping her tears. Father must be eating inattentively. In between Mother will be asking: Should I serve you anything more?

Being inattentive, my father will say- No, leave it. Mother will respond saying: You didn't eat anything? Everything is left out! Isn't it cooked well

Both of them will remain silent for a while as if who so ever speaks first has to go to the forest for twelve years. After a while mother will sob and say: why don't you go and call back your son and daughter-in-law.

Father will fume. I don't have any sons. I am nobody's father. Everybody is a cheater. Maybe I had sons at some point of time but I have got rid of them.

I couldn't tell *Rupashree* all these things though I wanted to. She saw me sitting quietly, and her eyes were filled with tears. I brought her close to me and wiped her tears.

After a while, *Rupashree* said: Let's go somewhere for a change. Let's go to Daringbadi or Konark, as I am sick and tired of this place. After marriage, we decided to spend seven days in Konark and watch the sunrise. We will visit Ooty for five days, but till now, we have yet to go anywhere. Her eyes were again filled with tears.

I remembered my dreams. *Rupashree* will go to the village after marriage and will stay there. She will say:

I don't want to work anymore as I must stay with my mother-in-law. My mother would bestow all her love and affection and cuddle her like a kitten, and *Rupashree* would prepare black tea for my father with lemon and ginger and serve him. She would learn about our culture and heritage from my mother like how to bake India cakes, traditional drawings of feet of Goddess of Wealth. Whenever I will return to the village on vacation, my mother would say: *Rupashree*: It's already midnight; why are you sitting here? My son is tired, go and take care of him.

I will take care of the rest of the things. You may go. When you weren't there, was I not taking care of the house?

When *Rupashree* will come to me, I will be in a deep sleep.

Are these dreams?

But to whom will I ask this question? Should I ask myself? I asked and got an answer from within: Go to your parents. Go back to your village. Hurry up!

I was startled.

Rupashree asked: Let me know when we will visit Konark. What are you thinking?

I said: Far from the Madding Crowd.

Rupashree laughed and said: Yes, only silence… The cool breeze of the Casuarina forest… Only you and me.

I inattentively said: This next second Saturday.

I was drinking tea in the morning when *Sapani* uncle arrived. I couldn't recognize him at first. He was a changed person now. Maybe he wasn't happy. Hardly there was any dialogue in between his sentences. I heard he worked in an ice factory in Calcutta; fell in love with the owner's daughter and brought her to the village. He is now working as a mason in the village.

I was surprised to see *Sapani* uncle. He sat down, lighted the hand-rolled cigarette, and asked: How are you?

I introduced *Rupashree* to *Sapani* uncle. *Rupashree* folded her hands with respect and went to prepare tea.

Sapani uncle said: So, yours is also a love marriage like mine, isn't it?

I smiled.

Sapani uncle said: In your adolescent age, you didn't smoke. Then how did you get into this love affair?

Sapani uncle was as excited as before. I simply looked at him and smiled. He was speaking in a mixture of English and Bengali ascent. He said: there was so much fun when I was living alone, but after I got married, things became different. After all, she belongs to a wealthy family, and adjusting according to my income is difficult.

I could guess that *Sapani* uncle had come to borrow money. But how did he come to know about my address in this city? He is a spendthrift right from his childhood. How much is he earning in a month as a mason? I was apprehensive. What will I do if he asks for money? *Rupashree* is very particular about this matter. Maybe she will bluntly refuse to lend money. If it's a matter of hundred or two hundred rupees, then I can give him.

Sapani uncle continued. He said Bengalis are inclined towards art. *Madhumita,* your aunt loves art and fell in love with me through my art. We are now in Bhubaneswar. I went to your house, but your father didn't speak to me, and your mother cried. I wanted to know what the matter was, so I came to meet you. Is it so that, like your elder brother, you are also not going to the village? In between, *Rupashree* came twice and heard our conversation. *Sapani* uncle was a little bit distracted while sipping tea. I didn't dare to look at his face.

Sapani uncle couldn't come down from his severity. He looked sad. I have never seen this expression on his face before. After that, he didn't speak a word to me. His face appeared pale and teary. While leaving, he only told this much *Rupashree*: It will be good if both of you can visit the village as your in-laws are eagerly waiting for you.

Sapni uncle left, and he didn't even turn back to look at us. After he left, I felt guilty. I felt like I had done a sin, which was difficult to counter. Why did *Sapani* uncle visit us? Did he come to tell me what he said?

I was sad.

That day, I sat quietly in the office. *Rupashree* asked me in the evening: When will we go for an outing? I remained silent for some time and then said: Let's go to the village for a fortnight.

Rupashree wasn't happy when she heard about the village. She said: Do we have so many days' leave to apply for? Let's go later. I said sternly: No, we will go tomorrow. Get ready by tomorrow morning.

Rupashree said: What about the office?

I was stern and said: If required, you will leave your job.

Maybe *Rupashree* couldn't understand. She looked at me astonishingly. She came close to me and said: I will do according to your wish. Father isn't keeping well. His asthma problem has increased, and he is coughing, so someone should be there to take care of him. Who is there to take care of him in this old age? You may go tomorrow. We will go together next time.

I was also thinking about my ailing mother, and about my father, who, irrespective of the mental turmoil what he was going through, was silently doing his work. Slowly I was becoming numb and hard like a rock. *Rupashree* came close to me and tried to divert my attention. She whispered: Are you angry with me? Please, try to understand the problem.

I was in my imaginary world and wasn't there with *Rupashree* then in the house. I imagined traveling by bus to my village, running through the fields, knocking at the door, and shouting at my mother to open the door. I wanted to tell her: Please, open the door and look, your youngest son has come. *Rupashree* was startled as she heard my caterwaul. She looked at me, but I couldn't look at her face. My eyes were filled with tears, and I was becoming weaker and weaker…. Lonely….Helpless.

The next day I left for the village.

I wrote the leave application for Casual Leave and handed it over to *Rupashree*, and said: I will stay in the village for a long time, so don't worry. *Rupashree* was silent, and I didn't pay any attention to that.

By the time I reached the village, it was afternoon. Every time I went to the village in the past, I could see my father at the bus stand, but he wasn't there today. Of course, I had suddenly planned to go to the village without informing them. The bus stand wasn't crowded, and I couldn't find any known people there.

I lifted the bag, hung it on my shoulder, and started walking. I felt as if I am an alien in that place. Those fields, the trees, and the surrounding looked new and unknown. I felt like I had come to that place for the first time.

When I reached the village, there was utter silence on the village roads. In that quiet afternoon, I heard a yogi singing a song full of melancholy that had the power to tremble the prevailing silence in the village.

I was distracted.

I remember that whenever my mother listened to the *Ektara* (songs played with a single-string musical instrument) played by the yogi, her eyes would fill with tears. I have never seen a yogi or a beggar returning from my house empty-handed. My mother would call the yogi, listen to his song, and feed him. She would give him rice and vegetables and ask: Yogi son! When will you come again?

I have noticed the tears in the eyes of the yogi. He would say: I will come again. When I come next, I will sing many new songs.

After the yogi leaves the village, for almost two hours, my mother would be remorseful. She would cry silently and wipe her tears.

I couldn't understand why my mother became sad and cried then, but I could understand it now.

I was tired and sat on the porch of our house. The yogi continued with his song.

You made a house in the middle of the forest…

Can't see anything except Ghanshyam…

Oh, Kahnu! My mind doesn't rest at home

Floating me in deep remorse…

Oh! Chintamani! You sailed away from me

I couldn't keep the balance of my mind

Oh My Kahnu

I fed you milk from my breast

And could see all this at this age

Couldn't understand what destiny has in store

Oh! My Kahnu…….

I turned back and saw my mother, leaning against the half-closed door and she was standing behind me. She wiped her tears and said: Yogi, you may go now. You can come some other day and sing as his father is sleeping. The yogi left. I was surprised for the first time; my mother told the yogi not to sing.

Mother said: Since how long are you sitting on this porch? Why didn't you call me?

I went in and changed my clothes.

My mother went to the kitchen to fry some spinach.

I asked: Is Father sleeping?

Mother said: Nowadays he isn't keeping well. Where is my daughter-in-law? Didn't you bring her along with you? Did you come alone?

I was startled and said: No, she didn't get leave from the office. She will come later.

Mother laughed. She sat beside me and asked: Is my daughter-in-law annoyed with us? You know your father very well. He thinks differently and is stubborn. You are also like your father. If you could have asked your father: Father, this is what it is and I wanted to do something like this. Would he have ever refused? Why did you do such a big thing without asking for it?

She wiped tears on her veil.

Two drops of tears rolled down my cheeks to mingle in the brass rice bowl. Mother said: What the elder one did, you did the same. Your father always says that my younger son is good as the elder one always kept himself away from others from his childhood.

After receiving the letter about your marriage, your father had never eaten properly. *Sapani* visited us recently, but he didn't speak to him. Sometimes at midnight, in his sleep, he blabbers about you. *Sapani* must have felt bad. I tried to make him understand that though the boy made a mistake, is it wise to take it so seriously? He said: My father has taught me to be stern. I may break, but I will never bow in front of anyone. My mother continued: I know what he says differs from his feelings. These are dialogues only. You know your father well.

I couldn't eat properly. I washed my hands, went to the backyard, and hiding myself, lit a cigarette. I was thinking about how to face my father. I have never spoken anything straight in front of my father. As time passed, I was feeling nervous.

I tried to sleep in the living room. The walls were covered with cobwebs, and our books on the rack were covered with dust. The faint smell of the bed made from a jackfruit tree, from mattress, and pillows in the room took me back to my childhood days. This is the place where my childhood is hidden. I stir through my past while being asleep in this room. Here rests the dreamlike my childhood days. The mornings of a painted book.

Once you open the windows, here lies the vast stretches of paddy fields. Through the windows of the room, I could see the fields. Through the windows comes the smell of paddy flowers during the flowering season; enters the fragrance of Mogra flowers. Slowly I was engrossed in these dreams. My eyes were getting loaded with sleep from soft and innocent palms.

Suddenly I saw my mother sitting beside me and looking at me surprisingly with some kind of unrecognizable eyes. I asked: Why are you looking at me in this way?

Mother said: Did you quarrel with my daughter-in-law?

Unprepared, I said: 'No'.

She became emotional, and her eyes were filled with tears. Maybe she thought that I was trying to hide something from her. She asked: Why didn't you bring my daughter-in-law with you? I can't believe your words.

I said annoyingly: Do you think that I am lying? So much work is in the office, so she didn't come. Mother said: You are trying to convince me, but what about your father? I smiled and said: I will explain it to Father. You won't understand how vital office work is. You will see how the father will be able to understand the problem.

My father felt a little better in the evening, and my mother told him that I had come to meet them. He was silent for a while. I was scared to go to him. In the meantime, my father had become very weak, and his face looked pale. He didn't say anything and sat quietly

After a while, I went near my father and touched his feet. I could see tears in his eyes. After some time, he said: Is my daughter-in-law having a lot of work in the office, or is she annoyed with me? His eyes were filled with tears or water?

Is he crying?

Is he not angry?

Why is he not scolding me? Why is he not saying that you are a disgrace to me? I am ashamed to call you my son. I disown you now. I don't have a son. I never had a son. I am a barren person.

Father wasn't saying any of this. He has become silent. Is he highly unwell? Is he annoyed with me?

Tears rolled down from his eyes as the water drops from the melting snow, but later he controlled himself.

After that, he didn't speak to me that night. My mother didn't talk to me much. By 9'O Clock the night, there was utter silence in the house. I could sometimes hear my father's coughing.

I got up from my bed and went to the courtyard. The house was never tranquil ever before.

I sat on my father's chair. The courtyard needed to be fully lighted as the moon sometimes hid behind the clouds in the sky. Does Father sit here and look at the hide and seek played by the light and darkness? He has spent his life in the game of hide and seek between happiness, sorrow, and dreams.

I looked at the sky. I rarely sat in the courtyard during my childhood days. During the summer, we slept in the yard, and my grandmother told us the stories of the wretched old demon, a ghost who had eyes like the wheels of a hack, and the handsome prince who rides a horse with wings. We will doze off before her story ends.

In the courtyard corner, my mother had planted the Mogra plant, which she brought from my grandfather's house that blooms throughout the year. Sometimes my mother looks at the Mogra flowers and cries, and when I ask her about it, she says she remembers her father. I remember the edentulous face of my grandfather that vanishes in a blink.

My father was sleeping, and my mother told me he hadn't sat on that chair for almost three months. He sat on that chair for nearly sixty years and faced all the ups and downs of life. The day my brother and sister-in-law left, he sat on the chair till late at night. He never cried or broke down. Instead, he said: What are you all thinking? Are you all thinking that I will be a burden to you? Never! Until I can do my work, I will never be a burden on anyone, and I will die the day I won't be able to do my work on my own.

He is still surviving with his parental ego. I was sitting on the same chair and crying. The sky was laden with stars after the moon set. There was no space even to drop a grain. I felt this beautiful canopy had been hanging above us for many years, and I could never enjoy its beauty so intimately.

I couldn't hear my father coughing. Maybe he was fast asleep. I decided to bring him and make him sit on the chair, keep my head on his lap and look at the beautiful sky. He will tell me the names of the stars in the sky. Here is *Pulastya, Angira,* … this one is <u>*Maricha.Dhuba*</u> and here is *Agasti…*

This star is of resolve and firmness. Be firm, truthful, righteous, and work hard. Never leave the path of righteousness.

He will point at the stars and say: This is the constellation of stars that brings rain. If it is in the right place, it rains heavily, the star of summer and famine. During the famine, this star shines brightly.

I will ask: Father, what is this star? What's the name of the star?

He will say: The learned and saintly men also don't know all-stars' names. If you take the total of all the creatures on this earth, their number will be less than the number of stars in the sky. They are uncountable. Who can count them? Is it possible to count them with human intelligence?

My brother would say: The scientists have already named the stars, and other than that, they were able to locate many new stars. Whatever father is saying are old tales.

But the villagers consult my father on all matters. As per my father's forecast, it rains, there is a flood, the crops ripen, and the lintel crops get infected by the insects.

How come the scientists don't know about it, but my father knows? How does he know about all these? My brother never argues with my father as he is too scared of him. He behaves like a thief in front of him.

I got up from the chair and went to my father's bedroom. He was sleeping, and I sat next to him quietly. I touched his forehead; it was cold. Maybe he doesn't have a fever now.

Feebly I called: Father… father.

He was silent.

I shook him again and called: Father… father …

I screamed: Father .. father. and called my mother and said: Why is father not responding?

My mother's shadow walked slowly, and sat near my father, stock-still.

I screamed and screeched like a lunatic.

I said: How can you sleep without telling me the names of all the stars? I know you don't know the names of all the stars. You are a liar.

Father, are you annoyed with me? Oh! Father… father. But he was silent.

Morning arrived keeping three of us in a triangle. I kept my head on my mother's lap.

My mother said: You aren't a small kid now. You have to perform all the rituals. Go and call *Hari* uncle.

I looked at her face. She looked like a goddess. She wasn't crying and was firm. I could realize that in the meantime, my mother has learned this quality from my father - how to be fervid in all situations.

I went out and called my uncles and others.

When they entered the house to carry my father, I could see my mother sitting there motionless and still. When I and my uncles and brothers lifted the dead body, she shouted: Don't touch him. He is still alive. Don't touch him…. And she held my father tightly. I tried to make her understand and said: Father is no more. Try to understand that. Why are you behaving like this?

She stared at me and asked like an insane person: Where did he go?

I cried but my mother didn't- she was stony.

Affter completing my father's rituals, I came with my mother to the city. *Rupashree* heard this, cried a lot, and said: You didn't allow me to see Father in his last days.

But my mother was silent and never spoke to anyone, not even me.

I asked her once: Mother, don't you like this place? I saw her smiling for the first time. She said: Take me to the village. Your father must be alone there and must be in trouble. Throughout his life, he struggled, and now, when he wants to live peacefully, you brought me here. Please, take me to the village.

I asked: How will you live alone there? Here the doctors are there to take care of your health; *Rupashree* is also there to look after you. Who will take care of you in the village?

She smiled for the second time and said: Don't worry about it. You know very well that your father is short-tempered. Please, don't keep me here. Take me back to the village.

Rupashree said: I think your mother has gone insane. Take her to the mental hospital and show the doctor.

I screamed: Shut up! Don't utter these words ever again for her. The consequences won't be good.

Rupashree became silent. I have never spoken like this

to her. *Rupashree* took it to heart, but I wasn't perturbed by that.

I spent that night alone on the terrace. My mother also didn't sleep that night and looked outside through the window. She was not thinking of anything else.

Early in the morning, Mother was ready to go to the village. I couldn't sleep properly at night, so I was asleep. She came, woke me up, and said: Get up! Won't you take me to the village? If you don't want to go, help me board the bus. I will go alone. The village is not that far.

My mother was never such stubborn.

I woke up, wore my clothes, and told *Rupashree* I am going to the village. *Rupashree* asked me: When will you return?

I said: Don't know.

Rupashree didn't say anything. I, along with my mother, left for the village. On the way, my mother didn't speak to me on the bus. Is she unable to remember her sons, for whom she always fought with my father?

As soon as we entered the house, my mother cried. I felt relieved, thinking that if she could weep, she could come out of her pain.

I had written a letter to my brother, so he was already there at home. My mother cried, looking at him. Both of us embraced each other and cried like our childhood days.

At night we slept along with her. My brother told her about various other things to divert her attention. He said about his elder son, who is very naughty and always asks about his grandmother.

She smiled for the third time and said: Why didn't you bring him along? Your father would have become happy. Listen, your father was never annoyed with both of you. You mightn't know, but he cries without anyone's knowledge when he scolds you. Try to understand him.

All of us slept together at night. In the morning, we couldn't find our mother. I went to the courtyard and saw my mother sitting on the chair my father used to sit on and was sleeping on. I ran towards her and could find out that she was no more. I brought her close, and my brother examined her and screamed like a kid: Mother!

She had a smile on her face. That was the fourth and last smile that we saw on her face after my father's death.

Rupashree, Sapani uncle and aunt, and my sisters and brothers-in-law went to the village. My sister-in-law and her children came from Delhi.

The funeral and rituals of my mother were performed. While taking the ceremonial dip, I mumbled: Mother, leave peacefully with Father in heaven. The river's water touched me gently, and I felt like my mother touched me and said: You are not a minor anymore?

At night I was sitting alone on that chair. The sweet smell of the Mogra flowers filled the atmosphere as the plants were adorned with the flowers. I felt as if my mother was smiling.

Rupashree came and touched my shoulder. Tears from her eyes dropped on my shoulder.

Rupashree asked: Are you annoyed? I was silent. I couldn't reply because I didn't know what to say. After all, there was nothing left within me to complain about.

Rupashree came closer to me and said: I will become a mother. Surprised; I rested my head on her chest and said: Will you be my mother… my mother?

Her bosom was wet with my tears. *Rupashree* was crying, and it had become an inconsolable childhood day.

From time to time, the sweet scent of the Mogra flowers engulfed us like mist.

Black Eagle Books

www.blackeaglebooks.org
info@blackeaglebooks.org

Black Eagle Books, an independent publisher, was founded
as a nonprofit organization in April, 2019. It is our mission
to connect and engage the Indian diaspora and the world at
large with the best of works of world literature published
on a collaborative platform, with special emphasis on
foregrounding Contemporary Classics and New Writing.

9 781645 604556